Jan 19

JUNIOR NINJA CHAMPION

JUNIOR NINJA CHAMPION

THE COMPETITION BEGINS

By
Catherine Hapka

HOUGHTON MIFFLIN HARCOURT
BOSTON   NEW YORK

hmhco.com

Logo design by Jason Cook.
The text was set in Minion Pro.

Library of Congress Cataloging-in-Publication Data
Names: Hapka, Catherine, author.
Title: Junior Ninja Champion : the competition begins / Catherine Hapka. Description: Boston ; New York : Houghton Mifflin Harcourt, [2018] | Summary: Five unlikely friends are brought together to compete in the first Junior Ninja competition, a televised contest of athletic ability based on the popular National Ninja Champion show.
Identifiers: LCCN 2017031539 |
ISBN 9781328710581 (paper over board)
Subjects: | CYAC: Athletes—Fiction. | Friendship—Fiction. | Reality television programs—Fiction. | Contests—Fiction. | Competition (Psychology)—Fiction. | BISAC: JUVENILE FICTION / Sports & Recreation / General. | JUVENILE FICTION / Social Issues / Friendship. | JUVENILE FICTION / Social Issues / Self-Esteem & Self-Reliance. | JUVENILE FICTION / Performing Arts / Television & Radio. | JUVENILE FICTION / Media Tie-In.
Classification: LCC PZ7.H1996 Jv 2018 | DDC [Fic]—dc23
LC record available at https://lccn.loc.gov/2017031539

Printed in the United States of America
DOC 10 9 8 7 6 5 4 3 2 1
4500710662

With many thanks to Allyssa Beird,
a ninja and a champion

One

IZZY FITZGERALD TIPTOED past the den. Her father and older brother were watching TV in there. She paused when she realized what they were watching. It was *National Ninja Champion.*

Oh right, it's the finals tonight, she thought.

She bit her lip, remembering the days when the whole family would watch that show together every week. Her mother had loved it . . .

But never mind. Izzy could catch the finals online later. Right now she needed to keep moving. She didn't want her dad to catch her sneaking out. Especially since she'd just finished being grounded from last time.

At least watching NNC will keep Dad and Charlie too

busy to wonder where I am, she thought as she crept toward the back door. *Not that they spend much time thinking about me anyway.*

She opened the door, lifting the handle slightly to avoid the squeak in the hinges. She closed it behind her just as carefully. As she bent down to grab her skateboard, which she'd stashed in the bushes right outside, Izzy heard voices at the back gate.

Yikes! She darted behind the dumb statue of some Greek goddess that her dad thought was so classy. Seconds later her stepmonster, Tina, came into view, dressed in her fancy new running shoes and designer sweats. Izzy's sixteen-year-old sister, Hannah, was with her. Hannah was laughing at something Tina had just said, even though nothing she said was ever actually funny.

Izzy touched her hair. She'd unbraided it just before sneaking out, so the purple streak her friend Jess had helped her dye into it was visible. Which meant she'd better not let Tina or her dad see it. They still didn't know about the purple streak. They said twelve was too young for a girl to start dyeing her hair.

Which is totally unfair, Izzy thought. *Especially since Tina spends half her time at the salon getting hers dyed that hideous shade of red.*

"Good run, sweetie," Tina was saying to Hannah, giving her a squeeze on the shoulder. "You'll be ready for that ten K for sure."

"Thanks for training with me, Tina." Hannah sounded happy and only a little out of breath.

"Anytime, sweetie. It's what we do, right?" Tina let out one of her tinkly little laughs. "Fitzgeralds are runners — that's what your dad always says."

Dad really did say that a lot, especially whenever he was trying to talk Izzy into joining the track team at school — just like Hannah and Charlie. Fitzgeralds are runners, Isabella, he'd say. You can't fight it.

Izzy wrinkled her nose, hating to hear him use her full name even in her head. She also hated to hear Tina use Dad's favorite phrase, since she wasn't even a real Fitzgerald — she'd only married Dad a year and a half ago. But she *was* a real runner. She and Dad had met at a half marathon.

Tina and Hannah seemed to stay out in the back courtyard forever, stretching and blabbing. But finally they went inside, and Izzy was free.

She dashed out the back gate and across the neighbors' pool deck, then vaulted over the fence to the street. Finally she dropped her board, kicking off and gliding down the hill toward the center of town.

Jess was waiting in the parking lot of the Hillside Shopping Center, lounging on a bench with her board at her feet and earbuds in. "You're late," she said, peeling out one bud.

"Sorry. Almost got caught." Izzy started to explain, but Jess waved it away.

"Whatever. Want to see a new move Tommy taught me?"

"Sure!" Izzy tried not to sound too eager. Jess was two years older, and Tommy was her boyfriend. Both of them went to Fairview High and were way cooler than anyone in the seventh grade at Izzy's snooty private school. Izzy felt lucky that Jess wanted to hang out with her.

Hillside was almost deserted, as usual, even though most of the stores were open until nine. Almost everyone had switched over to the fancy new mall out on the highway. But that was okay with Izzy. It meant she and Jess hardly ever got hassled about skateboarding or doing parkour here. Plus the weird two-level layout and the bumpy, weedy pavement made it more fun.

And parkour was the most fun Izzy had had since . . . Well, in a long time. It was all about fun — running, jumping, leaping over stuff, climbing walls, anything like that. She loved challenging herself that way, even when it was kind of scary. Maybe *especially* when it was scary.

Jess showed her the new trick, vaulting over the low wall at the edge of a walkway, using only one hand. They practiced that for a while and then did some of the usual stuff — leaping over parking barriers and decorative fences, various skateboard tricks, and more.

"This is boring," Jess said after Izzy landed a jump on her board. "I have an idea — let's do *that*."

She pointed to the sunken restaurant at the center of the shopping plaza. Izzy was confused.

"Do what? Go eat?" she asked.

Jess laughed and tossed her shaggy half-blond, half-green bangs out of her face. "No — the steps," she said. "Let's try skating down them." She grinned. "No jumping — you have to skate all the way down."

Izzy walked to the top of the steps. They were high and pretty steep, with a landing in the middle. "I dunno," she said. "Might be hard to make that turn. Plus you'd have to stop fast or hit the window at the bottom."

"Yeah. Cool, right?" Jess pulled a coin out of her pocket. "We'll flip to see who gets to go first."

Izzy hesitated, but Jess was already tossing the coin in the air. "Tails!" Izzy blurted out.

Jess slapped the coin onto the back of her hand. "Tails it is," she said. "You're up!"

Izzy swallowed hard and glanced at the steps. They suddenly looked even higher and steeper than before. But she never backed down from a challenge. Never.

Besides, she'd skated down steps before. Maybe not ones this steep or this high . . . But she couldn't chicken out in front of Jess. No way.

"What are you waiting for, Fitzgerald?" Jess said.

"Nothing." Izzy kicked off, holding her breath as the skateboard rumbled toward the top step — and then tipped off into nothingness. Her heart pounded and her hands went clammy as she stared down at the landing. But she stayed steady, arms out, balancing her body and keeping the nose of the board up as the back wheels found the edge of the next step and the next . . .

She hit the landing hard and skidded around the corner, grazing the wall with one elbow, but not slowing down. Only then did she get a good look at the second flight of steps. It was even longer than the first flight, and steeper, too. As the wheels left the ground, Izzy felt as if she'd just jumped off a cliff . . .

"Steer!" Jess shouted from somewhere above her. "You're going crooked!"

But Izzy was frozen, staring down at the ground rushing up toward her. She felt herself part ways from her board, and it was only when her shoulder hit the solid concrete wall of the stairwell that she snapped out of it, barely keeping her balance to avoid falling down the last few steps. Her skateboard, on the other hand . . .

CRASH!

The board hit the window and shattered it, glass flying everywhere. Izzy's whole body went cold, and she felt herself start to shake. What had she done?

"Whoa!" Jess exclaimed. "Let's get out of here!"

Izzy heard her friend's running feet. A second later, several people burst out of the restaurant.

"You!" a stern-looking woman shouted, pointing at Izzy. "Stop right there!"

Two

... AND NINETEEN, and twenty," Mrs. Santiago counted off. "Good job, Kevin! You're done for today."

Kevin Marshall lowered the arms of the rowing machine. "I could do another set if you want," he offered, feeling strong. Feeling good.

But Mrs. Santiago smiled and shook her head. "You know your mother's orders, Kev," she said. "We're supposed to stick to the routine your doctors prescribed."

Kevin's shoulders slumped, and he nodded. "Yeah, I know."

He knew better than to argue with his mother, even if she wasn't here right now. Especially about stuff like exercise or sports — or anything fun. He knew what she'd say if he did: *Don't sass me, young man. This is for your own good.*

Even Mrs. Santiago, who co-owned Fit Kidz gym with her husband, knew better than to cross Ms. Jacqueline P. Marshall. Everyone did.

Kevin packed up his gym bag. He'd started his workout a little later than usual today because of a student council meeting after school. It was the last one of the year, so he couldn't miss it.

Now it was just past six thirty, and the main room at Fit Kidz had almost totally cleared out as kids headed home for dinner. Only a couple of guys from the middle school soccer team were hanging out at one of the weight machines. Kevin watched them out of the corner of his eye, wondering what it would be like to be on the team with them. He'd just started playing peewee soccer back when he first got sick, and everyone had said he was a pretty good kicker.

But that was a long time ago. He told himself he was lucky that he was allowed to work out at Fit Kidz at all. It was better than nothing, right?

He glanced around the gym's main space, which had become very familiar over the past few years. It was a big, open room, with all kinds of fitness machines and other equipment. Overhead, a running track circled the whole thing like a mezzanine.

Slinging his bag over his shoulder, Kevin headed out

into the hallway. On the way to the exit were several doors. First he passed the yoga room, which doubled as a space for the little-kid tumbling classes. Across from that was the gymnastics room. A little farther along were the locker rooms. And finally, two more doors on either side. The one on the right opened into a maze of offices and storage closets and other stuff like that.

But Kevin kept his eyes on the door to the left. It was open, and he could hear shuffling sounds from inside. He paused, glancing in.

This was the teen room. Kevin had never been inside, but he checked it out whenever he walked past. Part of the room was taken up by boring stuff like weight benches and rowing machines. But there were also a bunch of cool, colorful obstacles — overhead bars, rings and nets, a climbing wall, a set of balance steps, a trampoline, a curved wall, and more. He could almost picture himself swinging and leaping through them all, just the way his heroes did every week on *National Ninja Champion* . . .

"Yo, Kevin! What's up? You catch the finals last night, man?"

Kevin snapped out of his fantasy. He hadn't even noticed Ty Santiago sweeping the floor under the climbing wall. Ty, tall and fit and muscular, with dark hair and tons of confidence, was in eighth grade and was the star of just about every team at Fairview Middle School.

Kevin knew right away what Ty was talking about

— the season finale of *NNC.* "Yeah, I saw it." Kevin didn't bother to tell him that he'd already watched the episode three times on the DVR. "It was great."

"For sure!" Ty started talking a mile a minute about the finals course. He dropped his broom and grabbed a set of hanging rings to demonstrate one of the moments he was describing.

Kevin was surprised. "Hey, we aren't allowed to mess around in here," he blurted out before he could stop himself. His eyes darted to the sign on the door beside him: AGES 14 AND UP ONLY.

Ty grinned and dropped to the ground, flexing his muscles. "Yeah, I know." He shrugged. "But my mom and dad own the place, remember? I like to sneak in here after hours and try a few ninja stunts sometimes."

"Really?" Kevin felt envy welling up in him. All those years of watching the show, wishing he could try even one of the obstacles . . .

"Yeah." Ty stepped closer, glancing out into the deserted hallway. "Hey, want to give it a go? Nobody's around."

Kevin gulped, his eyes darting toward the balance steps. They were just big blocks of wood with steeply sloped sides, but they looked almost magical to him. Images started playing in his head like a movie — an action-packed medley of all the ninjas over the years who'd leaped back and forth through a set of steps just like these. What would it be like . . .

But he shook his head. "I'd better not."

"Go ahead," Ty urged with a grin. "I'll keep watch and let you know if my parents are coming."

The word "parents" brought up an image of Kevin's own mother looking stern. He shuddered, trying not to imagine what she'd say if she knew he was even considering Ty's offer.

"Thanks, but I've got to go," he mumbled, turning and fleeing before Ty could say another word.

Three

MACK ATTACKS . . . . . .

MY BLOG ABOUT INTERESTING STUFF

By Mackenzie Clark, age 10½, nerdgirl extraordinaire! (← *that last word means fab!*)

Today: MACK ATTACKS . . . . . . Ninjas!!!

Hi again, loyal readers! So I just got home after dinner with my birth mom — as regular visitors to this blog know, she lives right across the street from me and my dads. As some of you also know, she works at an ad agency here in Fairview.

And tonight she had some **big** news to share that she

heard at work. It's about one of my all-time favorite shows, *National Ninja Champion*.

(Side note: OK, I know I have LOTS of all-time favorite shows, ha ha! But srsly, *NNC* is one of them — just search this blog for all the times I've talked about it!! It might not be SF or fantasy like most of my other faves, or have any aliens or time travel or magical powers in it at all, but it DOES have superheroes galore — they just happen to be the **real life** kind!)

But you probably know all about the show already, because you probably watch it, too. Everybody does! It's the coolest — men and women from all over the country compete on these awesome obstacle courses that test their strength, agility, and all that athletic stuff. I know I did like ten blog entries last season on the TWO, count 'em, TWO finalists from my very own home state, Johnny "Strongarm" Simpson and Tara "Tiny Torpedo" Warner. They were the tallest and shortest ninjas in the competition that year, isn't that funny?

Anyway, Tara looked like she was going to make it all the way through the finals course, but she went down on the second-to-last obstacle. It was one where the ninjas had to swing themselves across a pit and grab these super-skinny bars — she just missed the middle bar, oops! She says she'll be back next year, though — after she finishes stretching her arms a few inches longer, ha ha! (Ninjas always have a great sense of humor!)

Johnny DID finish the course — he almost fell on the Ring Swing obstacle in the middle, but he grabbed the last ring with two fingers and got himself back on track, it was amazing!!!! (He also had a really fast time and ended up coming in third overall, which is fab!)

But never mind that, I could talk about *NNC* all day, but I won't. Because I want to get back to the big news . . . and it's REALLY big!

THERE'S GOING TO BE A KID VERSION OF THE SHOW!!!!!!

OK, sorry for the shouting. But come on, that's huge, right? I don't know all the details yet, but I know a few things:

1. The competition is going to be open to kids ages 9 to 13.
2. It will begin filming midsummer — as in, just a few short weeks from now! (Okay, maybe more like a month and a half or a little more . . . but still!!)
3. One of the tryout locations is practically right next door to Fairview, in North Creek.
4. It's sure to be just as fun to watch as the grown-up version!

How **cool** is all that, right? I can't wait to see if any kids from my school try out! (As you all know, I'm allergic to exercise myself, ha ha, but I can't wait to cheer on anyone who does go for it!)

Watch this space for (**much!**) more about this . . .

Four

TY SANTIAGO SET the weight on the leg press a little higher, then flopped onto the bench. Kevin Marshall was a couple of machines over, plugging away at his usual boring workout.

Ty felt kind of bad for the kid. He looked athletic enough, other than being on the short side for a sixth-grader. But he was never allowed to do anything fun. Ty's mom said it was because Kevin had beat cancer a few years ago and his mom was just being careful. Still, Ty knew he'd go crazy if all he was allowed to do was the same basic, easy routine — stretches, bike, rowing machine — a few times a week for an hour or so.

That was why Ty had offered to stand lookout when

Kevin stopped by the teen room a couple of days earlier. He knew Kevin had wanted to say yes — the kid was an absolute *NNC* superfan. Too bad he'd chickened out.

But Ty was trying to focus on something else right then. He was doing his best to eavesdrop on his parents, who were talking to a man in a suit and a girl around Ty's age. The girl was built like a basketball player, tall and lean, with tidily braided dark hair and a sullen expression. She definitely wasn't on the Fairview Middle School team, though, or Ty would have known her.

". . . so we decided that if Isabella has enough energy for vandalism and mischief, she could put it to better use here. No sense letting her mope around her room the whole time she's grounded." The girl's father was tall and angular and looked sort of sour.

"I see." Ty's father said. He was just as tall as the other man but broader in the shoulders. Everyone said Ty took after his dad except for having his mom's greenish-hazel eyes. "All right, then, Isabella —"

"Izzy," the girl interrupted with a scowl, tugging on the hem of her black T-shirt. "Nobody calls me Isabella."

Ty traded a look with Kevin. The girl sounded pretty snotty.

"Izzy," Ty's dad said. "Okay. Do you want us to come up with a workout plan, or —"

"No, thank you." This time it was Izzy's father who

interrupted. "We want her to run. We Fitzgeralds are runners."

"Fitzgerald," Ty murmured. Why did that name seem familiar?

Then he remembered. Charlie and Hannah Fitzgerald were both on the track team at the private school across town. Charlie held the county record at four hundred meters, and Hannah ran anchor on the state champion relay team even though she was only a sophomore. Ty didn't run track himself—he couldn't, as the season conflicted with baseball—but he had mad respect for good athletes no matter what they did. He hadn't realized that the running Fitzgeralds had a younger sister.

He watched Izzy with new interest. She stood there with her head down and her arms crossed, staring at the floor while her dad and Ty's discussed the details.

Finally Mr. Fitzgerald left. "Okay, Izzy," Ty's dad said. "I'll show you the track."

"Fine, whatever," Izzy muttered. "Let's get it over with."

They were only halfway to the spiral steps leading up to the track mezzanine when another girl burst into the gym. She was almost as tall as Izzy and even skinnier, but she looked younger. Pale, gangly legs stuck out of oversize shorts, and she kept shoving her glasses up her nose. Ty had never seen her before.

"Hi!" she exclaimed in a high-pitched voice that made

her sound sort of like an overexcited chipmunk. "Are you Mr. Santiago?"

"That's me," Ty's dad said. "How can I help you, young lady?"

"I'm Mackenzie Clark." The girl actually stuck out her hand for Ty's dad to shake. "I heard you have a ninja gym here."

"Well, not exactly." Ty's dad looked her up and down. "We've got a few ninja-style obstacles in the teen room. But that's only for ages fourteen and up. How old are you, Mackenzie?"

She looked disappointed. "Oh, I'm only ten," she said. "Ten and a half, if you want to get technical. But I wasn't asking for me — see, they're doing a kids' version of *National Ninja Champion*, and I was hoping someone here might be trying out."

She went on to say something about a blog, but Ty was still stuck on what she'd just said.

"Whoa, did you hear that?" he asked Kevin, sitting up straight on the leg press. "Is this for real?"

"I don't know," Kevin said. "Let's find out!"

The two of them abandoned their machines and hurried over. "Hey, Dad," Ty said. He turned to Mackenzie. "Is *NNC* really doing a kids' show?"

"Yeah, I hadn't heard that," Kevin put in.

"My birth mom works in advertising, and the show is

going to start running ads here soon," Mackenzie said. "It's totally true!"

"Whoa!" Ty's mind spun. *National Ninja Champion* — for kids? He would be great at that! "Dad, this is huge! You've got to change the age limit on the ninja stuff so I can train for this!"

"Yeah," Kevin put in eagerly. When Ty glanced over in surprise, Kevin shrugged. "I mean, other kids might want to try out, too."

Ty noticed Izzy nodding as she listened. "It's a good idea, right?" he asked her.

She froze and then frowned. "Whatever," she said in a bored tone. "Will someone just show me the track so I can finish and get out of here?"

Five

"CHECK IT OUT," JJ Johnson said to his father, who was standing beside him looking up at the tree house in their backyard. "What do you think?"

His dad clapped him on the shoulder. "Looks good, son," he said. "Let's see you test it out."

"Sure!" A second later, JJ was scrambling up the home-made climbing holds he'd just installed on the tree trunk. It took him only seconds to reach the main platform. The tree house was really cool — he and his dad had been work-ing on it for almost four years. It had two separate levels, with a main room on the lower one and a reading nook above, where JJ kept his comics. There were also a couple of viewing platforms in the higher branches, and lots of ropes and ladders connecting everything.

JJ swung himself onto the edge of the platform and looked down. His dad shot him a grin and a thumbs-up. "Gotta go," he said. "Meeting your uncle to look over some estimates."

"Okay. Later." JJ waved as his dad strode off toward the big work truck parked in the driveway. The logo on the side read JOHNSON BROTHERS CONTRACTING: NO JOB TOO BIG OR TOO SMALL. Some of the letters in the words were made out of tools — a hammer for the *T* in "brothers" and a circular saw for the *O*.

JJ's sister, Jasmine, had designed the logo three years earlier. She was only eleven then, the same age JJ was now. Everyone said the logo looked as good as something a pro would do.

Then again, Jasmine was good at everything. She got straight As in school, compared with JJ's straight B-minuses. She was the youngest soloist ever in the church choir. She'd won prizes for archery and tennis and pottery at summer camp.

But JJ didn't mind all the attention she got. Better her than him. Sure, he was ordinary compared with Jasmine. But somebody had to be ordinary, right?

He glanced down at the climbing holds, wondering if he could fit any more on the trunk. The holds were a much more interesting way to get up to the tree house than the old rope ladder. He couldn't wait to show his friends.

JJ glanced toward the Cohens' house next door. There was no sign of the twins, but someone else was loping across the backyard — Ty Santiago, who lived three doors down.

Ty spotted him and waved. "Yo, Jake, hey!" he called.

JJ was surprised. He and Ty didn't know each other that well, even though they'd lived in the same neighborhood all their lives. For one thing, Ty was a year ahead of JJ in school. Plus they didn't have much in common. Ty was into sports — *really* into sports. There were articles about him on the school website almost every week.

JJ liked sports just fine. He liked watching football with his dad and uncle and cousins. He liked shooting baskets in the twins' driveway or playing kickball at recess. But that was just messing around, not being a real athlete like Ty.

"What's up?" he called. "Hang on, I'll come down."

"No, it's cool — I'll come up there." Seconds later, Ty was clambering up the trunk using the new climbing holds. When he reached the platform, he was grinning. "Really dope climbing wall — uh, I mean tree. You put those grips in yourself?"

"Yeah, started yesterday after school and finished today." JJ shrugged. "No big deal."

"Okay. But listen, you're good at building stuff, right?"

Ty waved a hand around at the tree house. "Because I need your help."

"Sure. What's up?"

"You know the show *National Ninja Champion*?" Ty asked.

"I've seen it," JJ said. "Cool show."

He didn't watch much TV, preferring to spend his screen time playing video games. But he caught an episode of *NNC* now and then. He always ended up thinking he should watch more regularly—though he usually forgot.

His eyes widened as Ty told him about the junior ninja show. "... and one of the tryout locations is right over in North Creek," Ty finished eagerly. "And trust me, I'll be there! I was made for that show, you know?"

"You're really going to try out? Wow. I've never known anyone on TV before." JJ paused, considering that. "Well, except for the time my sister was on the local news when her essay won an award."

Ty didn't seem too interested in hearing about Jasmine. "So listen," he said, drumming his fingers on the wooden platform. "I almost have my parents convinced to let younger kids train on the ninja obstacles at the gym."

JJ nodded. Ty's parents ran the only kids' gym in town. JJ had been there once or twice for birthday parties, but he'd never noticed any ninja obstacles. "Cool," he said.

"The problem is, they're worried that the stuff is all scaled for teenagers, who are mostly taller. They say it'd be too expensive to hire someone to adjust it." Ty grinned at JJ. "That's where you come in."

Six

IZZY WAS HATING LIFE as she plodded around the Fit Kidz track for the zillionth time. "Fitzgeralds might be runners," she muttered, "but *this* Fitzgerald thinks running is *boring!*"

Finally she finished the prescribed number of laps. This was only her fourth day of coming straight to the gym after school, but she'd already learned not to try to cut out early. She'd tried that on day two and discovered that the Santiagos were keeping a closer eye on her than anyone ever did at home.

She grabbed her bag from the alcove at the top of the stairs. Then she jogged down, wishing Jess were there. The spiral staircase would be perfect for parkour.

"See you tomorrow, Izzy," Mr. Santiago called as she left. He was over at one of the exercise machines, helping that short black kid she'd met on the first day. Well, she hadn't *met* him, exactly, but he'd been there with the owners' obnoxious son, Ty.

Thinking back to that day reminded her of the big news that nerdy ten-year-old had brought. Were they really doing a kids' version of *NNC*?

Izzy thought about that as she headed down the hall. She slowed her pace when she reached the teen room and glanced in through the half-open door. She'd noticed that there were some ninjalike obstacles in there. At the moment, there was nobody inside.

Her eyes darted up and down the hall. Not a soul in sight. So she slipped into the room, checking out the obstacles. There was a set of balance steps, just like the ones on TV. A jungle of rings and bars and ropes and other climbing stuff. Even a Crazy Cliff, the tall, curved wall that had appeared on every *NNC* course since the beginning. Izzy eyed it, wondering if she could make it to the top . . .

A clatter of feet and a babble of voices hit her from outside. Yikes! If anyone caught her in here . . .

She ducked behind a pile of mats, hoping that no one came in. To her relief, the voices soon faded away toward the exit.

Izzy knew she should scoot before she got caught for real, but she couldn't resist another look around. Once again, she wished Jess were there. The two of them could have so much fun in this place.

She dropped her bag and wandered toward the balance steps. They were brightly colored blocks of wood set a few feet apart in two staggered rows. The idea was to jump from one steeply angled step to another without having to touch the ground in between. It was a great test of balance and agility—not that different from parkour, now that Izzy thought about it. Probably easier, actually . . .

Before she knew it, she was jumping onto the first step, pushing off with her foot as she started to slide down the steep face of the wooden block. She hit the second step just right but was a little low on the third one. For a second she thought she might fall. Instead, she pushed off harder, hitting the fourth step near the top and having no trouble hitting the fifth and final one.

"Score!" she said softly, lifting her arms in victory as she landed on the mat at the end of the row.

"Whoa!" someone said behind her.

Izzy gasped and spun around . . .

Seven

TY STARED AT IZZY, annoyed and amazed at the same time. "What are you doing in here?" he demanded.

"Wow," Kevin said from beside him before Izzy could respond. "Where'd you learn to do balance steps like that?"

The girl's blue eyes darted from one boy to the other. She settled on Ty, scowling.

"What's it to you?" she said.

Ty crossed his arms. "Can't you read? You have to be fourteen to come in here."

"At least for now," Kevin added softly.

That's the point, Ty thought. If this girl got in trouble for sneaking in here, his parents were less likely to go along with his plans. He almost had them convinced. Especially after JJ and his dad had come in yesterday to talk to them. Ty figured it wouldn't take long to adjust the equipment for shorter, younger kids. School would be out for the summer pretty soon, and then he could train full-time for his awesome ninja victory.

"So have you done ninja stuff before?" Kevin asked, taking a step into the room. "You looked like one of the National Ninja champions or something just now! I'm Kevin, by the way."

Izzy was silent for a second, looking Kevin up and down. "Izzy," she said at last. "You like *National Ninja Champion*?"

Kevin shrugged. "I've seen every episode at least once, usually more," he admitted, wandering over to touch the balance log, a spinning cylinder of brightly painted wood.

"Really?" Ty asked, distracted for a second. He raised his hand for a high-five. "Dude! I mean, I knew you were a superfan, but that's hardcore!"

"I guess." Kevin slapped him a weak high-five. "The thing is, the show first came on when I was — when I was sick."

"Sick?" Izzy echoed.

"He had cancer," Ty told her. Then he glanced at Kevin. "I mean, that's what my parents said. Right?"

"Yeah. I had plenty of time to watch TV while I was

laid up getting treatments and stuff. Actually . . ." Kevin's voice trailed off, and he shot the other two kids an uncertain look.

"What?" Izzy asked, sounding curious.

Kevin cleared his throat. "Um, this might sound crazy, but watching the show gave me extra strength to fight my cancer. At least that's how it felt, you know?"

"I get it," Izzy said with a nod. "Some of those ninjas have pretty inspiring stories. Like the guy who competed the first time while he was homeless —"

"Or that woman with the prosthetic foot," Kevin added. "There have been some cancer survivors, too."

Ty didn't say anything. He knew what they were talking about — sort of, anyway. He usually got up to grab a snack when the ninja biography segments came on, or he fastforwarded through that part if he wasn't watching it live. He preferred the action of the actual competition. Now he sort of wished he'd paid more attention . . .

Just then he heard movement behind him. Spinning around, he saw his parents standing in the doorway. Uh-oh — busted!

"We — we were just —" he stammered.

His father ignored him. "Sorry for eavesdropping, kids," he said, gazing thoughtfully at Kevin. "We couldn't help hearing what you were just saying."

Ty's mother nodded. "You never told us that before, Kevin — about being so inspired by *NNC*."

Ty knew that look—his mom was touched by Kevin's story. "Yeah," he put in quickly. "The show totally helps people. It could help even more if you let us train here."

"It really does inspire people," Izzy put in. "I mean, maybe I haven't seen every episode like some people . . ." She shot a small smile at Kevin. "But I watched it a lot with my whole family the first couple of years it was on. And after my mom left . . ." She paused and shrugged. "I guess watching it sort of made me forget she was gone. At least for an hour."

Ty raised his eyebrows. He didn't know much about Izzy, although his parents had told him she was at the gym because she'd accidentally broken a window downtown. They'd mentioned parents—as in two. So what was she talking about?

Ty's mom looked even more touched. "Wow."

"Uh-huh." Izzy shrugged one shoulder. "I think that's why I got into parkour and stuff, you know? It helps me focus on fun stuff instead of bad stuff."

Ty's parents traded a look.

Ty stepped toward them. "See?" he said. "You guys love helping kids, right? Isn't that why you started this gym? You could help even more by letting kid ninjas train here. It would be totally inspiring or whatever, right?"

His dad chuckled and held up his hands in surrender. "All right, all right," he said. "You've convinced us, okay?"

"We were leaning toward doing it anyway," Ty's mom

added. "So let's make it official. Starting tomorrow, the ninja area is open to kids age nine and up."

"But only with supervision — no messing around at random," Ty's dad warned. "Your mom and I will keep an eye on things in here until we can find a coach. And we'll have to be careful until your friend JJ and his dad can help us make those adjustments we talked about."

"I'll send a message to our email list right now, and print out a new sign for the door," Ty's mom said with a smile. "We can start signing up members of our new junior ninja team right away."

"You can put me first on the list," Ty said, puffing out his chest.

"And me second," Izzy added. At Ty's look of surprise, she shrugged. "I figure I can train after I finish my daily run."

Ty frowned at her. Izzy didn't seem to take anything that seriously. She was the type who'd probably get cut by any of his coaches within the first week. In other words, not the kind of kid he'd pictured training with . . .

Then again, she'd probably get bored and drop out before long. Anyway, Ty decided not to worry about it. He had much more interesting things to think about — like how much fun it was going to be becoming the first-ever Junior Ninja champion!

Eight

MACKENZIE WOKE UP feeling extra psyched on Saturday morning. She jumped out of bed and rushed over to her laptop, quickly typing in a short blog post, updating her readers about the day's plans — she was going to Fit Kidz to check out the new junior ninja team.

How cool was it that the Santiagos had agreed to host a team! She spent most of breakfast telling her dads all about it. They were excited, too, even though Daddy Jim wasn't into sports at all. He called himself a classic indoor nerd — skinny, pale, glasses, just like Mackenzie herself.

Papa Kurt was a little more interested. He often watched *NNC* with Mackenzie and loved telling stories about playing kickball and going camping as a kid.

And of course, both of them thought it was great that she was so excited. They even teased her about trying out for the ninja team herself.

"As if," she whispered with a smile a little while later as she pushed through the glass doors with the Fit Kidz logo on them. Okay, maybe she'd fantasized about it a tiny bit. But Mackenzie Clark — a ninja? The whole idea was crazy, right? She was allergic to exercise, just like Daddy Jim. Still, it would definitely be fun to watch and blog about the whole process.

When she reached the ninja room, the new team was already there. Okay, it wasn't much of a team — just Ty, Izzy, and JJ so far. Mackenzie had watched their first workout after school a couple of days earlier. She'd already sized up their strengths and weaknesses in her mind, based on her years of careful observation and analysis of *NNC*. That made her an expert, she figured.

At the moment, Mr. Santiago was helping JJ move a small trampoline closer to the balance log. Izzy was chugging from a water bottle and watching Ty, who was messing around on the climbing structure.

"Hi, Mackenzie," Kevin called. He was perched on a pile of spare mats, watching the others.

Mackenzie waved and walked over. She liked Kevin — he was smart and friendly and just as big a fan of *NNC* as she was. It was too bad his mom wouldn't let him be on the ninja team. But at least he could help out by coaching the others.

"Hey, Mackenzie!" Ty called out. "Put this on your blog!"

He leaped up and grabbed the overhead bars. He swung across the whole row of bars and did a flying dismount at the far end.

"Whoo!" Mackenzie cheered, clapping. "That was awesome! Do it again and I'll get some pictures!"

Ty started the bars again. As Mackenzie snapped a few shots with her phone, Kevin frowned. "We already know you can do the upper-body stuff, Ty," he called out. "Weren't you going to start working on balance exercises today?"

"Whatever." Ty finished with another dramatic dismount — this time on one foot. "I can balance. See?"

JJ snorted with laughter. "Extra points!" he shouted.

Just then Mr. Santiago's phone buzzed. He glanced at it. "I need to deal with something, kids," he called out, already hurrying toward the door. "Take five until I get back."

As soon as he disappeared through the door, Izzy leaped onto the teeter-totter. "I can balance, too — check it out," she said with a smirk.

JJ looked worried. "Hey, Ty's dad said to take five."

"I did — five seconds." Izzy jogged effortlessly across the slender tilting beam.

"Wow, she's good," Mackenzie said to Kevin, snapping

a few more photos as Izzy did a ballerina-style spin and then went prancing back across the teeter-totter in the other direction.

But Kevin was still frowning. "Yeah, Izzy has great balance. But these guys can't just work on the stuff they're good at, or they'll never make the show."

Mackenzie thought about Ty muscling his way across the overhead bars. And Izzy leaping from one balance step to another. And JJ scrambling up the climbing wall, as nimble as a monkey.

"Good point," she said. "Maybe you should talk to them about that." Without waiting for Kevin to respond, she stood and clapped her hands. "Hey guys! Listen up! Your coach here" — she pointed to Kevin — "wants you to switch it up, okay? Like, maybe Izzy should try working on strength training for a while, and JJ and Ty could do balance exercises."

"Oh yeah?" Ty flexed his muscles, looking annoyed. "You're not actually our coach, you know, Kevin."

"Yeah," Izzy said, shrugging. "I don't need a coach."

Mackenzie winced. The two of them sounded kind of cranky. Maybe this was why her dads were always advising her to think a little more before she shared her ideas.

"Yes, you do need a coach," Kevin was saying to the others. "Otherwise you'll blow it on your weak spots."

"I don't have weak spots, okay?" Ty bragged.

"Oh yeah?" Kevin stood up. "Is that why you fell off the balance log before you got halfway across yesterday?"

"I was just playing around." Ty rolled his eyes. "Anyway, if you're such an expert, let's see you try something. Seriously, dude. I bet you can't last three seconds on that stupid log."

"Wanna bet?" Kevin took a step toward the obstacle. "If I make it across, will you shut up and listen to my ideas?"

Mackenzie gulped. Things were feeling a little tense, and it was all her fault.

Ty was already crossing his heart. "Deal," he said with a wicked grin.

Izzy nodded. "I'm in. Let's see what you've got, *Coach*."

JJ looked a little worried. "But Kev, I thought you weren't —"

He didn't bother to finish. Kevin was already jumping onto the end of the balance log, which was shaped like a tree trunk lying sideways and was free to spin on the metal bar that ran down its center. The log tilted abruptly under his weight, and for a second Mackenzie thought he might wipe out right away.

But Kevin stuck out his arms, windmilling them as he fought for balance. The log stabilized, and he took a step forward — then another. Soon he was almost at the other end . . .

But Mackenzie barely saw his dismount. Because

someone had just walked into the room — a petite woman dressed in shorts and a tank top; she had curly brown hair and a tattoo of a firecracker on her bicep.

Mackenzie's jaw dropped. "Whoa!" she exclaimed. "It's the Tiny Torpedo!"

A second later Ty's father reentered. He towered over the woman, who was an inch or two shorter than Mackenzie.

"That's right," Mr. Santiago said with a smile. "Meet Tara Warner — the Tiny Torpedo!"

JJ looked a little confused. But Ty and Kevin were both nodding, and even Izzy looked impressed. "She was on *NNC* this past season," Kevin told JJ. "She did great!"

"Oh." JJ smiled. "Nice to meet you, Ms. Torpedo."

"Ms. Warner," Mr. Santiago corrected with a laugh.

The woman laughed, too. "Just call me Tara, okay?" she said, her brown eyes twinkling. "So who are you all?"

Mr. Santiago's cell phone buzzed again. "Oops, excuse me — I'm sure you kids can introduce yourselves to your new coach." He hurried out of the room.

Coach? Mackenzie's head spun with this news. She couldn't wait to break it on her blog!

"Wow, you're really going to coach the Fit Kidz ninja team?" she exclaimed, rushing over. "Oh, I'm Mackenzie, by the way — nice to meet you!"

"Ditto." Tara shook her hand. "Interesting training outfit, Mackenzie."

Mackenzie glanced down at her planet-printed sundress

and favorite purple flip-flops. "Oh, I'm not on the team," she said with a laugh. "I'm just here as a fan. And to report about the team on my blog."

"Cool. I bet these guys love having a fan here to cheer them on — I always do!" Tara smiled at the others. "Let me guess — you must be Ty?"

"How'd you know?" Ty said. "Oh wait — did you see my picture in the paper after we won States last month?"

Tara grinned. "Nope. Saw your picture in your parents' office just now, though."

"Oh, right." Ty looked a little deflated, but he pointed to the others. "Anyway, that's JJ, and that's Izzy. Oh, and Kevin."

"Nice work on the balance log, Kevin," Tara said. "You'll be a real asset. Can't wait to see what the rest of you can do."

Mackenzie's eyes widened as she realized that Tara thought Kevin was on the team. That wasn't a huge surprise. He was dressed in workout clothes, and she'd just seen him tackle a ninja obstacle like a pro. Mackenzie waited for Kevin to explain, but he didn't say a word. Neither did the others, so Mackenzie kept quiet, too.

Meanwhile, Tara clapped her hands. "Okay, team," she said. "Let's get started!"

Nine

JJ TOOK A DEEP BREATH and surveyed the balance steps. It was the team's third day training with Coach Tara, and JJ had been having a great time so far. But these steps? Not fun. He hadn't made it any farther than the second one before wiping out.

"Go for it, JJ!" Tara called. "You can do it!"

"Yeah, you'll get it this time," Mackenzie said from her viewing spot atop the pile of extra mats. She added a bunch of sciencey stuff about biomechanics and gravity, the way she often did.

"Enough, Mack," Izzy said with a snort. "Science is for school, not the gym."

JJ grinned as Mackenzie stuck out her tongue at Izzy.

"Okay, here goes nothing," he said. Then he jumped onto the first step. Right away he felt his foot skidding down the smooth, slanted surface. He leaped for the next step, but caught only the lower edge. He skidded off, landing on his hands and knees.

"You okay?" Tara asked.

"Yeah." JJ jumped to his feet and brushed himself off. "I'm fine."

Tara clapped him on the back. "Okay, take a breather. We'll try again in a few. Ty? You're up next."

Ty stepped forward, swinging his arms around to loosen up. JJ wandered over and leaned against the mats where Mackenzie was sitting. She'd brought her laptop today so she could update her blog in real time.

"It's okay," she told him. "You'll figure it out."

"Maybe." JJ shrugged, not too worried about it. During the first two days of training he'd discovered that he could climb just about anything. He was also great at swinging around on the rings and ropes and overhead bars. He'd even mastered the Loco Ladder, an obstacle where you had to climb a sheer wall by moving a pair of metal pegs up a set of holes in the wall. It required tons of upper body strength, since you had to hold yourself in place with one arm each time you moved the other peg up. Plus it was tricky, since the holes were easy to miss. Even Ty still hadn't made it the whole way up, but JJ had done it on his third or fourth try. He was proud of himself for that.

So what if he couldn't do any of the balance obstacles? He didn't want to be a TV star or a famous blogger like Ty or Mackenzie. He didn't care about being the best at stuff the way Izzy did. JJ was only in this whole ninja thing for the fun of it. He wasn't sure he'd even bother going to those tryouts. But he kept trying, mostly to make Tara happy. She was a great coach, and JJ was sure she'd help Ty make it onto the show. Maybe Izzy, too.

JJ glanced over at the rope bar, where Izzy was struggling to hold on as she climbed up one of the ropes. She was the opposite of JJ and Ty. She could skip through the balance steps as if they were nothing, and she was great at the balance log and teeter-totter, too. She also wasn't bad at swinging along from ring to ring and stuff like that. But climbing straight up a rope was harder for her, and she hadn't made it more than two or three holes up the Loco Ladder yet. And of course, none of them had come close to making it to the top of the Crazy Cliff — not even Ty.

A frustrated shout grabbed JJ's attention. Ty had just wiped out on the last balance step.

"This is stupid!" Ty hopped up and kicked the step. "The ones on the show probably won't be as steep as these anyway."

"Think again, Ty." Tara shook her head. "These steps are pretty standard. If anything, the ones on the show might be tougher."

"Whatever," Ty muttered, scowling.

Tara shrugged. "Get your head together, okay?" she advised him. "I'm going to spot Kevin on the Loco Ladder now. Kev? You're up!"

Kevin had been working on the teeter-totter, which he was already pretty good at from what JJ could tell. But now he hopped down and followed Tara over to the Loco Ladder. Kevin looked nervous as he glanced up at it.

"You can do it!" JJ called encouragingly.

"Whoo, Kevin!" Mackenzie added, pumping her fist. Then she glanced at JJ. "I hope he gets the hang of it soon. There's a Loco Ladder on almost every *NNC* course, so they'll probably do it on the kids' version, too. At least that's what Tara says."

JJ nodded. "He'll get it. He's strong enough. He just needs to work on his eye."

They both watched as Kevin jumped up and grabbed the pegs, which were on the lowest pair of holes. He tensed his muscles, then jerked the left-hand peg out and up, then shoved it into the next highest hole.

"Awesome!" Mackenzie yelled, snapping a photo with her phone.

Kevin rested for a second. Then he pulled out the right-hand peg. But this time the peg missed the next hole. He let out a yell as his left hand slipped off its peg and he crashed to the floor.

"You okay?" Tara asked, helping him to his feet. When Kevin nodded, she smiled. "Good. Try it again."

The whole group worked hard for the next half hour or so. Finally Tara checked her watch and said she had to go.

"We'll pick up again tomorrow," she said. "Great job, everyone!"

But as she hurried out, Izzy was frowning. "What's great about it?" she grumbled. "My nick might as well be the Noodle-Armed Ninja."

Mackenzie and Kevin chuckled.

"Nick, as in nickname?" JJ said.

"Yeah. A lot of the ninjas on *NNC* have nicknames," Mackenzie told him. "Like the Tiny Torpedo — get it?"

"Oh, right." Now JJ vaguely remembered that. He grinned. "So, like, Ty's nickname could be the Power Ninja."

"I like it!" Ty flexed his muscles like a bodybuilder.

"And Kevin's could be the Kevinator," Mackenzie suggested. "Or wait — how about Special K? That's catchy, right?"

She started to type on her laptop. Kevin looked alarmed. "You're not putting that on your blog, are you?" he demanded.

"Sure. My readers will love it."

"No!" Kevin sounded firm. "You can't mention my name at all. Promise you won't, okay?"

"Why not?" JJ asked, perplexed by the anxiety in his voice.

"My mom would flip her lid." Kevin shook his head. "She doesn't even know I'm doing this."

JJ was surprised and a little curious. His parents had thought it was a great idea for him to join the ninja team. Even Jasmine was supportive, at least sort of. Sure, she probably thought he was going to try out for the TV show and be a big star. After all, that was what she would do . . .

He shook that off, still confused by Kevin's comments. But the other three kids were nodding as if they knew all about it, so JJ didn't ask more questions. It really wasn't any of his business.

Ten

TY NARROWED HIS EYES, glaring at the Crazy Cliff. It looked huge.

"Take your time — and focus," Tara said somewhere behind him.

Ty hardly heard her. When the coach had announced that they'd start out working on the Crazy Cliff today, Ty's first reaction was relief. He'd been afraid that she might make him practice balance stuff, the way she had yesterday.

After that, though, his relief had been taken over by a twinge of nerves. Sort of like the ones he'd had right before the big game at States.

But he'd triumphed then, and he planned to triumph

again now. All he had to do was channel his nerves into action. That was what Coach Channing always said.

"Aargh!" Ty shouted, bursting into a run.

The Crazy Cliff was the most iconic obstacle on the *NNC* course — and one of the simplest. It was a high, slightly curved wall. The idea was to leap or run up it far enough to grab the lip at the top and pull yourself up.

Ty had seen countless ninjas attempt the Crazy Cliff, and he'd seen quite a few of them fail. Just today, Kevin had tried several times and come nowhere near getting to the top. No wonder — the kid was short. But Izzy was as tall as Ty, and she'd failed, too. She'd come pretty close on her third attempt, but her fingers had just missed grabbing the lip at the top of the wall.

Failure wasn't an option for Ty, though. He'd never failed at anything in his life, and he didn't plan to start now.

He flung himself at the cliff, stretching up . . . up . . . up . . . His chest hit the smooth surface, and his hands grappled for the lip. Instead, they found only more wall, and he felt himself sliding down . . . down . . . down . . .

"Man!" he cried when he landed. "This is impossible."

JJ nodded. "It's one of the obstacles we didn't know how to adjust for shorter kids without building a whole new cliff," he told Tara. "Maybe that's why we're having trouble."

"Maybe." Tara shrugged. "But think of it this way.

We don't know how tall the cliff will be on *Junior Ninja Champion*. If you can beat this one, whatever they throw at you on the show should seem like a piece of cake."

"Ooh, good point!" Mackenzie said. She was there again, as she'd been for just about every practice so far. "Maybe I'll say something about that on the blog. I can use the video I just shot of Ty wiping out."

"What?" Ty blurted out. "No way! Delete that video!"

"Why?" Mackenzie glanced at her phone. "I can use it in a before-and-after montage. You know — when you finally conquer the cliff."

Climb that cliff! Ty could almost hear the chant from the crowd, which happened on every episode of *NNC*. But he shook it off.

"You have to delete it," he insisted. "Seriously, do it now! Or else!"

"Or else what?" Izzy smirked. "Are you going to beat her up?"

"Kids . . ." Tara began.

Ty folded his arms over his chest. "I'm not kidding around, Mackenzie," he said. "I want you to delete that video."

Mackenzie rolled her eyes. "It's not that big a deal, Ty," she said. "I'm sure you'll conquer the cliff soon. You probably just need to adjust your approach —"

She started babbling about angles and velocity and a bunch of other stuff Ty didn't understand. But he wasn't really listening anyway. He was imagining what the guys from the basketball team would say if they saw that embarrassing video. Or the kids from his traveling soccer league, for that matter . . .

He interrupted Mackenzie, who was still talking. "Oh yeah? If it's so easy, I'd like to see *you* do it!"

Mackenzie looked startled. "Huh?"

"Yeah." Ty glared at her. "Go ahead — I dare you."

"If she does, will you let her post that video?" Izzy asked with a grin.

"No way," Ty said. "But if she fails, she has to delete it."

"That's not fair," Kevin said. "You have to give her something if she makes it."

Ty glanced up at the top of the cliff. "Fine, she can post it if she makes it. No way will she make it, though."

He smirked at Mackenzie, expecting her to back down. But she grinned and hopped to her feet. "Deal!" she exclaimed.

Ty blinked in surprise, but Kevin and JJ were cheering Mackenzie on. Even Izzy was smiling.

Only Tara looked slightly concerned. "Are you sure you want to try this, Mackenzie?" she asked. "Don't let the others goad you into it if you'd rather not."

"No, it's okay." Mackenzie kicked off her flip-flops, tugged up the waistband of her shorts, and stepped to the bottom of the Crazy Cliff. "I want to test out my theories anyway. Maybe what I figure out can help the team."

"Climb that cliff! Climb that cliff!" Kevin and Izzy chanted as Mackenzie took her spot.

Ty didn't say anything. He just wanted her to hurry up and fail already. Then he'd know that video was gone.

"Okay, let's do this!" Mackenzie cried.

She took off, running straight at the cliff, her gangly arms and legs pumping. Ty held his breath as she flung herself upward, hoping she didn't break something. Her long arms stretched up — and grabbed the lip!

"Go, Mack!" JJ shouted.

She dangled for a second and looked as if she were about to drop. But then Ty watched in amazement as Mackenzie kicked herself a little farther up the wall, flipping herself up and onto the top of the obstacle.

She'd just conquered the Crazy Cliff — on her first try!

Eleven

KEVIN WAS IMPRESSED as he watched Mackenzie do a little victory dance atop the Crazy Cliff. That had been amazing! She'd conquered the toughest obstacle in the gym — the toughest one on *National Ninja Champion* — on her first try!

Coach Tara was grinning from ear to ear. "Get down from there before you fall off, girl," she called. "We need to talk!"

Ty looked stunned. "I can't believe she did that!"

"Get ready for that video to go viral, Power Ninja," Izzy joked.

Mackenzie climbed down the ladder on the side of the Crazy Cliff. "Don't worry, Ty," she said. "I'll still delete the video if you want. You can give me an interview for the blog instead."

"Really? Thanks!" Ty looked relieved. "That's cool of you."

"Never mind that." The Tiny Torpedo had an eager gleam in her eyes. "Mackenzie, you've been holding out on us!"

"What do you mean?" Mackenzie slid her skinny feet back into her flip-flops.

"I mean we need you on this team," Tara said. "How about it?"

Kevin's eyes widened in surprise. Mackenzie looked surprised, too.

"Me? A ninja?" She laughed. "No way."

"Yes, way," JJ said. "That was supercool how you just flew up there!"

"But ninjas are athletes," Mackenzie protested. "I mean, I love the show and all. But the most athletic things I ever do are walk my dog and ride my bike to the comic book store."

Tara shook her head. "You have to be an athlete to do what you just did."

"Yeah," Izzy agreed. "You looked like a natural."

"Okay, but that's just one obstacle," Mackenzie protested. "It doesn't mean I can do a whole ninja course . . ."

"Most people can't do a whole ninja course. You have

to start somewhere . . . and conquering the Crazy Cliff on your first try is a pretty good start!" Tara said. She insisted on seeing what Mackenzie could do, and Mackenzie finally agreed to try, though Kevin could tell she still thought Coach Tara was being silly. "We'll let you try some other obstacles tomorrow," Tara told her. "Talk to your parents tonight and get their permission first." She glanced at Mackenzie's feet and smiled. "And no flip-flops, please."

The next day, Kevin and the others watched as Tara put Mackenzie through her paces. She was a little weak on the overhead bars, and she couldn't do the Loco Ladder at all. But she was almost as good as Izzy on the balance obstacles, and her long arms helped her out with the ropes and rings.

By the time she finished the balance steps, Mackenzie was smiling. "Okay, this is just as much fun as it looks on TV," she said as she jumped off the last step. "I'm sure I won't make the show or anything, but at least being on the team will get me backstage at tryouts, right?"

JJ laughed. "That's the competitive spirit," he joked.

Kevin chuckled along with the others, but he wasn't feeling that happy. Actually, he was envious. Maybe Mackenzie wouldn't make the show. But he was sure she'd be allowed to try out — unlike him. He still hadn't told his mother or brother that he was hanging around after his workout to train as a ninja. He hadn't told Tara the truth yet, either.

Luckily, Mr. and Mrs. Santiago didn't seem to realize he was actually on the team now instead of just hanging around watching like before. At least not yet . . .

He tried not to worry about that as the workout continued. When they finished for the afternoon, Tara pulled some papers out of her bag.

"These are for you," she said, handing one sheet to each of the kids. "It's all the info you need about the tryouts — when, where, all that good stuff. Look them over, share them with your parents — and get ready! Tryouts are just one month away!"

Everyone except Kevin let out a whoop. He was staring at the handout Tara had just given him. He gulped, knowing he had to talk to his mother soon. She had to let him try out!

Ty clapped him on the back. "You okay, buddy?"

Kevin forced a smile. "Sure. Can't wait for tryouts."

As he walked home from the gym, Kevin did his best to psych himself up. He would just have to explain to his mother how important this was to him. How careful Tara was, warming them up and cooling them down properly. How much fun it was to be part of a team . . .

He was smiling as he pushed through the back door into the kitchen. But his smile faded when he saw his younger brother. Darius was sitting at the table with a large white bandage wrapped around one arm.

Their mother was bending over him, her face a mask of

worry. "Oh, Kevin!" she exclaimed. "Will you look at this? Thank the Lord it isn't broken!"

"What happened?" Kevin asked.

Darius sighed. "I fell when we were doing chin-ups in gym."

"Can you believe it?" Their mother threw her hands in the air. "Second-to-last day of school, and he goes and gets injured!"

Kevin's heart sank. No way could he talk to his mother about being a ninja now.

No way.

Twelve

LOOKING GOOD, MACKENZIE!" Izzy hollered. Then she grinned at Kevin, who was resting beside her on the pile of mats. "You can tell it really bugs Ty when Mack beats his time."

It was a week before tryouts, and Izzy was in a good mood. Tara was having them run mini-courses. Balance steps, then tire swing to cargo net, then Loco Ladder, then balance log. Izzy had already taken her turn and had done pretty well, though she'd been slow on the ladder as usual. She always panicked a little on that one, especially near the top. But she was trying to ignore that feeling, and today she'd mostly done so.

"Good job!" Tara called as Mackenzie finished with a

flourish. "You're really making up for lost time, girl! You have the fastest time so far."

"See?" Izzy whispered, elbowing Kevin. "Look at Ty's face."

Kevin smiled weakly, barely glancing in Ty's direction. Izzy frowned. What was up with this kid? Usually he was one of the most enthusiastic members of the team. But today he was grumpier than Stepmonster Tina when she ran out of her favorite coffee beans.

"What's with you?" Izzy asked.

"Huh?" Kevin was watching JJ start his turn. "Nothing."

"Don't give me that." Izzy swung her legs around so she could stare at Kevin. "You're acting like a freak. You nervous about tryouts or something?"

Kevin finally turned to look at her. "No," he said softly. "Because I'm not going to tryouts."

"What are you talking about?"

Kevin bit his lip. "Promise not to tell anyone?"

"Sure, whatever. I'm no snitch." Izzy couldn't imagine what would make him look so freaked out. But how bad could it be?

Kevin glanced around, but nobody was paying attention to the two of them. Tara, Ty, and Mackenzie were focused on JJ as he started the Loco Ladder, grunting each time he moved a peg another hole up the wall.

"I still haven't told my mom I'm doing this," Kevin said. "I'm afraid she'll run into Mr. or Mrs. Santiago and find out that way, but so far she hasn't. I've got to tell her myself, but I'm afraid she'll say no." He shook his head, looking sick. "Actually, I'm *sure* she'll say no."

"Why would she say no?" Izzy shrugged. "I thought my dad and stepmom would freak out, too, since I'm only supposed to be running here. But when I told them about it last week, it was no biggie."

She thought back to that night at dinner. It still surprised her how proud her dad had looked. And how Charlie and Hannah had both said they wished they weren't too old to try out. Even Tina had asked a bunch of not-too-annoying questions and seemed kind of interested.

"It's definitely going to be a big deal to my mom." Kevin grimaced, picking at a loose thread on the mat. "She acts like I'm made of glass or something."

"Oh, right — because of the cancer thing?" Izzy shot him a sidelong look.

"Yeah. Anyway, that's why I'm not going to try out," Kevin said. "That way I don't have to tell her, and at least maybe I can keep working out with you guys."

"Are you serious?" Izzy exclaimed. "What kind of ninja are you, anyway?"

"No kind of ninja. That's my point."

"No, seriously!" Izzy said. "If I only did what my family wanted, I'd never have any fun at all." She thought about it for a second. "Actually, I wouldn't even be here."

"Okay — but I'm not you," Kevin said.

Izzy thought about being insulted, but she decided against it. "Look, your mom must have signed that permission form thingy so you could be here at the gym without her, right? Everyone has to have on one file — I remember Mr. Santiago telling my dad about it that first day. Tara said that's all we'll need for the local tryouts — remember?"

Kevin blinked. "Did she say that?"

"Uh-huh." Izzy smiled. "So you can just go for it and try out — your mom never needs to know." She considered that. "Unless you make the show, I mean. And we can deal with that later if we have to, right?"

Kevin looked uncertain. "I guess . . ."

"What's the worst that could happen?" Izzy said. "Anyway, we need you. You can't let the rest of the team down."

"I guess," Kevin said again. He still seemed uneasy, but Izzy had the feeling that her teamwork comment was starting to convince him. He wanted this so badly — probably even more than Ty. How could he even think about letting his family hold him back? Izzy didn't get it. But she wanted to help him if she could.

Thirteen

"WOW, LOOK AT THIS CROWD!" Mackenzie pressed her nose against the window of the Fit Kidz van. It was the day of tryouts. Mrs. Santiago was driving the whole team — including Tara — to North Creek.

Mackenzie was so excited she could hardly stand it. This was really happening! She'd brought her tablet and phone along in her gym bag so she could update her blog throughout the day. She snapped a photo of the North Creek gym and the hordes of people milling around outside.

JJ leaned past her for a look. "There are tons of kids here!" he exclaimed. "Are they really all trying out?"

"Looks that way," Tara said, glancing back from the front passenger seat. "Don't let it psych you out, though."

"Right," Mrs. Santiago added. "Remember, you kids have the best coach in the biz helping you."

"Whoo! Go Tiny Torpedo!" Mackenzie cheered, while JJ and Kevin clapped a little. Izzy was staring out the window, and Ty had that focused look he got sometimes, and he didn't seem to be paying attention.

Mrs. Santiago dropped them off at the front door, promising to rejoin them after she found a parking spot. Tara led the way inside. It was even more crowded in there.

Tara stood on tiptoes to peer over the crowd. "We need to figure out where to check in," she said. "Anyone see a sign?"

A kid stepped toward them. "It's over there," he said, pointing. He was almost as tall as Ty, with bright red hair and freckles. "Better hurry. They're starting soon."

"Thanks," Tara said. She waved Mackenzie and the rest of the team after her. "Follow me, and don't get lost."

The next few minutes were pretty chaotic. They waited in line and signed their names on a long list. The woman at the sign-in table pointed them toward an arched doorway.

"You can take a look at the course in there," she said. "There's a marked warm-up area—the run order will be posted there soon. Have fun, and good luck!"

"Are you nervous?" Mackenzie whispered to Kevin as they followed Tara toward the arch.

Ty heard her and looked over. "I'm not," he said. "I'm going to own this course!"

"Well, I'm terrified," JJ said. "But I guess it's too late to back out now, right?"

"Definitely." Mackenzie grinned at him. "It's going to be fun, no matter what happens."

Her smile faded when she got her first look at the course. It looked enormous!

"Whoa," Kevin said. "That Crazy Cliff has to be higher than ours."

"And I can barely make it up ours!" JJ added with a grimace.

"It's not any higher," Tara assured her. "It just looks fancier. You guys can do this. I promise."

"She's right." Ty raised his fist. "We're ninjas! We can do this!"

"We're ninjas!" Mackenzie shouted along with JJ and Kevin. Izzy rolled her eyes, but joined in the fist bump.

"Yeah — ninjas," she said. "We can totally do this. So let's go get warmed up already."

Fourteen

T Y'S HEART JUMPED when he heard the announcer call his name. "I'm up!" he said, jumping up from the bench where he'd been pounding water. It was hot in the gym, and he was already sweaty from his warm-up.

Tara clapped him on the shoulder. "Ready?"

"I was born ready." Ty cracked his knuckles, channeling the competitive energy he always got before a game or other contest. He was warmed up. He'd studied the course — seven obstacles, that was all he had to conquer. Then he'd be on the regional semifinals show, one step closer to being crowned the Junior Ninja champion at the finals!

"Good luck, Ty!" Mackenzie called. The others added their well wishes, but Ty hardly heard them. He was the first of their team to go, and he figured that was the way it should be. He'd show them how it was done. Who knew? Maybe one or two of them might even make it onto the semifinals show with him. But even if they didn't, they could come to the taping and cheer him on.

Tara walked out of the warm-up area with him. Tons of people were milling around outside the course borders. But inside, it was empty and waiting. Waiting for him.

Ty fist-bumped with Tara one last time. Then he stepped forward, taking his spot on the mat in front of the balance steps. There were only four steps — easy. He glanced past the steps at the second obstacle, a pair of tires hanging from chains high over the mats. The idea was to jump up and grab the first tire, then swing it until you could grab the second one. The dismount would be tricky, since there was no rope or cargo net to grab. But Ty was pretty sure he could do it.

A man and a woman were standing beside the balance steps. The man held a clipboard, and the woman had a stopwatch.

"Begin whenever you're ready, Mr. Santiago," the man said.

"Thanks." Ty rubbed his hands on his thighs and glanced at the steps again. He could almost hear his baseball coach in his head: *Let's do this thing, boys!*

Let's do it, Ty told himself. Then he leaped forward . . .

The first balance step was a little steeper than he

expected. His foot skidded, and for a second he had the horrible feeling he might fall on the very first obstacle. He had to focus! He'd been so busy thinking about the tire swing that he'd taken this one for granted!

"Aargh!" he shouted, pushing himself forward and up with all the strength in his body.

He hit the next step just right. Whew! After that, the third and fourth steps went fine, and he landed squarely on the mat on the far side.

Ty rested for only a second, aware that the stopwatch was running. He was glad Tara had made him practice those stupid balance steps so much. How embarrassing it would have been to wipe out right away!

Putting that out of his mind, he stepped onto the small trampoline at the base of the second obstacle . . .

The tire swings were hard but fun. After that came a crooked balance beam, and again Ty silently thanked Tara for making him work on his balance. He wobbled a couple of times but got across pretty quickly.

Then came the Loco Ladder. Ty had practiced that obstacle over and over again until he could beat it every time, and today was no exception — he could hear loud cheers as he reached the top and swung down on the dismount rope.

He shook out his arms as he stepped onto the trampoline to mount the next obstacle, a set of hanging rings. It was probably the simplest exercise on the course. But as soon as he began, Ty realized it was harder than it looked. The rings didn't swing as freely as the ones at Fit Kidz, and they were set wider apart. And the rings themselves were thicker, which made them harder to grip.

"Yaaaah!" Ty grunted as he finally made it to the last ring. The dismount mat looked impossibly far away, but he swung with all his might and managed to grab the rope.

Whew! That had been tough . . . Ty was winded, but he didn't dare slow down. He'd already lost some time on the rings. If lots of kids finished the course, their times would determine which ones made the cut.

Besides, there was just one more obstacle before the Crazy Cliff at the end of the course. Ty had conquered the Crazy Cliff at home weeks ago, and he knew he could find the strength to make it up this one, too.

But there was one more balance obstacle to deal with — something Tara called log steps. It was a set of three balance logs, like the one from Fit Kidz, but thinner and set parallel to one another — sort of like the rungs of a giant ladder lying on the ground. The idea was to leap across, using the logs as steps. Tara had explained that it was tricky, since the logs could all rotate freely, and it was easy to lose your balance and wipe out.

"You can do this," Ty whispered to himself. He jumped forward, and his right foot hit the middle of the first log. He felt it start to roll, and he pushed off hard — a little too hard . . .

"Oof!"

Ty hardly realized what had happened until he landed on the mat beneath the logs. A groan went up from the onlookers.

"It's okay, Ty!" someone shouted — Ty was pretty sure it was Mackenzie's voice.

He punched the air with frustration, glancing up at the Crazy Cliff. So close!

Tara hurried to meet him as he stood and left the course. "Good job, Ty," she said. "I'm proud of you. Your time was great! Hardly anyone's made it past the logs so far, so you've still got a good shot at making the show."

"Really?" That made Ty feel better. "Wish I could've finished, though." He glared at the logs.

Fifteen

JJ CHEERED AS Izzy skipped across the balance beam as if it were nothing. She was the third member of the team to attack the course. Ty had come close to finishing, and so had Kevin — he'd even made it through the Loco Ladder, which was his hardest obstacle. But then his hand had slipped on the middle ring on the next obstacle and he'd ended up sprawled in the safety net.

Izzy was just finishing the Loco Ladder when Kevin came over to where JJ was watching. "You're next, right?" Kevin asked him.

JJ's heart skipped a beat. But he tried not to let it show. "Yeah. Right after Iz finishes."

"Cool." They both watched as Izzy stepped to the ring obstacle. She leaped up and grabbed the first ring. Kevin winced as she lost her grip with one hand. "Ty was right," he told JJ. "Those things are hard to hold on to!"

"I'll remember that." JJ forced a smile. "If I make it that far, that is."

He still couldn't quite believe he was here, getting ready to try out for a national TV show. How had that happened? He'd never pictured himself actually going to the tryouts. But there had never seemed to be a good time to back out. Tara and the rest of the team assumed that JJ was trying out, so here he was. Terrified.

Izzy had managed to regain her hold. She swung from one ring to another, using her long legs to help propel her through the air. JJ thought she was going to make it . . . but she fell a little short on the dismount. Her foot skidded off the mat, her fingers missed grabbing the net, and she toppled backwards into the safety net.

"Darnit!" she shouted as she popped up.

"Good job," JJ said, hurrying over and offering a hand to help her climb out.

She ignored it, crawling out on her own. "Whatever — thanks," she muttered. "I wish I'd made it to the end."

JJ nodded. The second-to-last obstacle was a balance one, which was Izzy's specialty. She probably could have mastered the log steps easily. Then all she'd have to face was the Crazy Cliff, and as Tara had pointed out after taking a closer look, it was a couple of inches shorter than the one at Fit Kidz.

"Heads up — get over there." Tara gave JJ a shove toward the start of the course as she hurried to meet Izzy.

JJ obeyed, although his legs felt like jelly. "Good luck, Mr. Johnson," said a man with a clipboard. "Begin whenever you're ready."

"Thanks." JJ blinked, wondering why the lights shining down on the course had to be so bright. Tara had explained that the tryouts were being filmed so the producers could use excerpts on the show, but that didn't seem like a good enough reason to blind the competitors. JJ could barely see as he leaped toward the opening obstacle.

Somehow, though, once his foot touched down on the first balance block, he sort of forgot about the lights. And that everyone was looking at him. And that he was auditioning for a TV show. He just had fun, the way he did every day at the gym.

He skipped through the balance blocks, almost over-jumping on the second one but recovering quickly. The tire obstacle was fun, and as he landed, JJ decided that he should add a couple of tires to his tree house setup.

The balance beam went well, too. After that came the Loco Ladder. That started out okay, but the distance between the sets of holes seemed awfully long, and by the time JJ reached the second-to-top holes, his arm muscles were aching. He came a little short on one of the final holes and tumbled down into the net.

"Oh well," he whispered to himself as he glanced up at the wall towering over him. Then he broke into a smile. "That was really fun!"

Sixteen

MACKENZIE HUNG ON to the ring with all her strength. "Good thing I have long fingers," she muttered as she swung her legs, imitating how she'd seen Izzy do it. She grabbed the final ring, then swung herself onto the mat, flinging herself forward to grab the net on landing.

Whew! She'd made it through the obstacle that had taken out two of her teammates. But there was no time to pat herself on the back. The log steps were next, and even Ty hadn't been able to finish that one, though a few ninjas from other gyms had done it.

Mackenzie closed her eyes for a second, picturing the tall redheaded kid who had given them directions earlier.

He'd done the course about fifteen minutes earlier. He'd wiped out on the logs, and Mackenzie was pretty sure she knew why—he'd leaned forward too much. Angles and vectors and fulcrums flew through her mind, and she opened her eyes. She knew what to do.

"Go for it, Mack!" JJ hollered from the sidelines.

Mackenzie glanced that way. The whole team was there, cheering her on, along with Tara and Mrs. Santiago. Mackenzie grinned and shot them a thumbs-up, hoping that Kevin was remembering to take lots of photos with her phone as she'd asked.

Then she focused on the logs again. After one last deep breath, she jumped . . .

Her foot barely touched the first log before she was pushing off again, using the log's movement to help propel her. The second log was trickier—Mackenzie landed a tiny bit short, and the log rolled back rather than forward. But she flung her upper body ahead to counterbalance and managed to make it onto the third log. Then all she had to do was complete the arc onto the landing mat.

"Go, Mackenzie!" Tara shouted.

Mackenzie was panting already from the effort of the course. She looked up at the Crazy Cliff. No matter what Tara had told them, it looked *high!*

But she was still too pumped up to worry about it. She raced forward, elbows flailing in what Ty called her "chicken sprint." Flinging herself up the wall, she thought about friction and energy and . . . before she knew it, she was hauling herself up over the lip!

The crowd went crazy, but Mackenzie hardly heard it. She leaped to her feet and did a happy dance. That had been fun!

It was only after she rejoined her teammates that Mackenzie found out what this meant.

"Only eight kids completed the whole course, including you," Tara told her with a smile. "You know what that means, right? You're going to be on the show!"

Mackenzie gasped. "For real?" But her brain was already calculating the numbers, telling her that Tara was right. She was going to be on *Junior Ninja Champion*! She couldn't wait to tell her readers.

But first there was a wait as a few more ninjas took their turns at the course. After that, the judges huddled, figuring out who else had made the show.

"I have to make the cut," Ty muttered, pacing back and forth as they all waited for the news. "I have to!"

"You will," JJ assured him. "Hardly anybody made it across those logs."

"And your time was really good," Mackenzie added. "Anyway, I hope all you guys make it. I don't want to do it alone!"

"You won't be alone," JJ assured her. "We'll all be there cheering you on, no matter what. Right, guys?"

"Sure," Kevin agreed. Izzy shrugged and nodded,

though she seemed distracted. Ty was pacing again and didn't respond at all.

"Looks like they're ready," Tara said, nodding toward the judges as they emerged from a back room.

The head judge started by thanking everyone for taking part. Then she read off the list of kids who were invited to be on the regional show. Mackenzie had made it, as expected — and so had Ty, Izzy, and Kevin!

Only JJ had missed out, though he was on a list of alternates who would be called in case any of the competitors couldn't make it. "Sorry, bro," Ty told him with a clap on the back.

JJ shrugged. "It's cool. I wasn't even expecting to do as well as I did," he said in his usual easygoing way. "Congrats to all of you, though! I'll be there to cheer you on for sure."

"Awesome," Izzy said, grinning from ear to ear, which, Mackenzie realized, she hardly ever did. It almost made her look like a different person.

It made Mackenzie feel even happier to see her friends so excited. Her feet started tapping, and then her arms and shoulders started bobbing, and before she knew it, she was doing another happy dance.

And this time, all her teammates joined in.

Seventeen

KEVIN FELT GREAT as he danced wildly with his friends. He'd made it! Even better, most of the team had made it, too! All that hard work had paid off, and Kevin was proud of himself and the others. He tried not to think too much about what came next. Why ruin this moment with reality?

After all the names were read, the judge had another announcement. "Contestants and alternates, please stop at the table in the lobby and pick up a show packet on your way out," she said. "See you in two weeks for the filming!"

"What's a show packet?" JJ asked as the team gathered up their stuff to leave. Mrs. Santiago had already hurried off to bring the van around.

Tara slung her backpack over her shoulder. "Paperwork for the show," she said. "There'll be a release and a contract and a list of rules. Oh, and probably a number your parents can call to set up a time to film your package."

"Package?" Izzy echoed.

"That's what they call the little film segment that plays before a contestant's round," Mackenzie explained before the coach could respond. "You know — it usually says where the ninja is from, how they got their nickname, how they got into ninja-ing — stuff like that." She grinned at their looks of surprise. "I told you, I'm a nerd — I know everything!"

The others laughed, but Kevin could barely force a weak smile. Releases? Film packages? That settled it. There was no way he'd be able to slide through again without telling his mother that he wasn't just cheering his friends on at the gym, but was actually on the team himself.

Izzy nudged him with her elbow. "You okay?"

"Sure." Kevin shot a look at Tara just ahead. "I'm fine."

Izzy narrowed her eyes at him, but she seemed to realize that he didn't want to say anything else just then. Meanwhile, Tara had reached the archway leading into the lobby, which was packed with kids and adults. She stood on tiptoes to peer around.

"I have an idea," she said. "Why don't you kids go wait outside for the van. I'll grab everyone's packets. Easier than all of us trying to push our way through this mess."

"Good idea," Izzy said, heading for the nearest exit. "Come on, guys."

When they got outside, there was no sign of the van. A long line of cars crept past the front of the gym, picking up young ninjas.

Ty shaded his eyes, peering off toward the parking lot. "Looks like Mom's stuck in traffic," he announced. "Should we walk over and meet her?"

"Nah, we have to wait for Tara anyway." Mackenzie flopped onto a bench. "Besides, I'm beat. Being a super ninja is tiring!"

Ty flexed his biceps. "Not me. I feel great!"

"You should feel good, too, JJ," Kevin said glumly. "Because you'll probably get my spot when I have to drop out."

Everyone turned to stare at him. "What are you talking about?" Ty asked.

Kevin sighed. "It's my mom. She thinks I can't do anything just because I had cancer. I haven't told her I'm on the ninja team."

Mackenzie's eyes widened. "Are you serious?" she exclaimed. "But why not? I'm sure if you just explain —"

"She won't listen," Kevin interrupted. "Anyway, it's too late. Maybe if I'd told her right away . . ."

He let his voice trail off. Closing his eyes, he tried to imagine what might have happened if he'd told her the truth from the start. Would she have freaked out as he'd thought, or would she have listened?

Oh well, he thought. *At least I got to prove to myself that I could do it.*

Eighteen

IZZY WINCED AT the raw emotions flashing across Kevin's face. The kid was an open book. They all could read how dejected he was. Izzy felt sort of guilty about that. After all, she was the one who'd encouraged him to keep this secret from his mom.

She hung back as the others gathered around Kevin.

"How can we help?" Mackenzie asked him.

"Yeah," JJ said. "Maybe we can come up with a plan or something."

"I could ask my folks to talk to your mom," Ty offered.

Kevin made a face. "That won't work. They'll probably

be mad at me, too. I never exactly told them the whole story, either."

Mackenzie grabbed his hand. "You should just talk to your mom," she urged. "I'm sure she'll understand if you explain how important this is to you—"

"Not necessarily," Izzy put in, thinking of her own father and stepmother. Sure, they'd been surprisingly cool about this ninja thing, but they were totally unreasonable about most of the stuff she did. "Some parents just don't understand. It's like they totally forgot what it was like to be our age."

"Shhh," Kevin said. "Here comes Tara. I don't want her to know about this, okay? At least not yet."

"You heard him, guys," Izzy said. "Start talking about something else."

She felt terrible for Kevin. How were they going to fix this?

Izzy was still thinking about it when they got back to Fit Kidz. "Home sweet home," Mrs. Santiago sang out as she cut the engine. "Well done today, gang. Can't wait to see what you do next!"

"Me, neither," Ty declared as he jumped out of the van.

Soon he and his mom had disappeared inside the gym. Mackenzie grabbed her bike and pedaled off, yelling something about being late for dinner.

"See you guys tomorrow," JJ said.

"Yeah, I guess." Kevin gave a little wave and started walking away.

Izzy wanted to say something to him, but she wasn't sure what to say, so she just waved back.

She dug into her bag for her earbuds, but couldn't find them. That was weird. She rarely went anywhere without them.

Still, there hadn't been much time to listen to music today. She decided to go inside in case she'd left them in the gym that morning.

When she entered the ninja room, Tara was there doing chin-ups. She dropped to the floor when she saw Izzy.

"What's up, Iz?" the coach asked cheerfully. "Just getting a little workout in. You guys inspired me today — I need to stay fit for next season!"

"That's cool." Izzy glanced around and spotted her earbuds on the pile of spare mats. "Just forgot these." She hurried over and grabbed them.

"Okay. See you tomorrow." Tara smiled. "We need to be ready for the show, and we've only got two weeks to do it! I hope you're ready for more hard work."

"Sure." Izzy hesitated, thinking again about Kevin. What was the point of him working so hard if he wouldn't get to be on the show?

Tara noticed her expression. "What?" she asked. "Are you okay, Izzy?"

"Yeah, I'm fine." She wished she could tell Tara about

Kevin's problem. But he didn't want her to know, and Izzy was no snitch. "I was just, um, wondering if you're part of a team like ours."

Tara's face lit up. "Of course!" she exclaimed. "That's a big part of what I like about the ninja community. We're all like one big team." She grinned. "Although my smaller team from *my* gym is especially awesome . . ."

She talked a little more about some of her teammates. A few had been on the show with her. Others were still working hard, trying to get good enough to make it through tryouts.

It was interesting, but Izzy had trouble focusing. "I like our team, too," she said when Tara stopped talking.

"You kids are great," Tara said. "You're all very different, but you're really supportive of one another — that's important."

Izzy kicked at the edge of the mat. "Yeah, I guess."

"It's true," Tara insisted. "I don't have scientific proof or anything, but I'm pretty sure having friends behind you helps a ninja's performance. That's why finding the right team is important. Friends can help you do anything. That's what they're for, right?"

"Sure," Izzy said.

But what if that friend doesn't want your help? she wondered. *Maybe being a real friend means figuring out how to help anyway.*

Nineteen

THE DAY AFTER TRYOUTS, Ty was psyched up to keep training. Now he knew what he needed to work on, and he was ready to put in the hard work. The balance stuff wouldn't beat him next time!

He headed for the ninja room as soon as he arrived at the gym. Nobody was there yet, not even Tara. So he decided to start stretching without them. He glanced at the balance log.

"You and me, dude," he muttered, giving it the evil eye. "Just gotta warm up first . . ."

He was doing some easy stretches when his dad came in. "Ty," he called. "I need to talk to you."

"Sure." Ty hopped to his feet. "What's up, Dad?"

His father held up his phone. "Just got an email from the Tri-County League," he said. "It's got the final schedule for this season."

Ty nodded. Tri-County was the traveling soccer league he played on every year. He'd been so busy with his ninja training that he'd almost forgotten it would be starting soon. Now that he remembered, he felt a shiver of anticipation. Ty loved all sports, but he looked forward to this soccer league all year long.

"When are tryouts?" he asked eagerly.

"That's the problem." His father's brow furrowed as he glanced down at his phone. "They're two weeks from yesterday."

"Okay." Then Ty blinked as he realized something. "Wait! That's the same day as the *JNC* taping!"

"Exactly." His father shook his head. "I already called, and there's no makeup date. Either you show up to try out that day, or you're out."

"What?" Ty cried. "But that's not fair! Did you tell them about the show?"

His father nodded. "They were sympathetic, but they said no exceptions." He put a hand on Ty's shoulder. "You're going to have to make a choice, son."

Ty's head spun. This was horrible! He'd been on the soccer league for the past five years, and he was pretty sure he'd be one of the top picks this time. That meant lots of playing time, maybe a championship . . .

But then there was the Junior Ninja championship. Ever since he'd first heard about it, Ty had known he was destined to win that title. He couldn't do that without triumphing in the finals, and to get there, he first had to make it through the regional show in two weeks. He knew he could do it. But was it worth giving up a whole season of soccer for a few minutes on the ninja course?

Just then Mackenzie rushed into the room, followed by JJ. "Where's Tara?" Mackenzie exclaimed. "We're ready to rumble!"

JJ laughed and high-fived her. A moment later Kevin wandered in.

"Hey!" Mackenzie greeted him cheerfully. "Did you talk to your mom?"

"No," Kevin said shortly. He turned away to put his bag down.

Ty grimaced, feeling bad for Kevin. But he felt even worse for himself. How was he supposed to decide what to do?

Twenty

A FEW MINUTES LATER, Kevin wiped his palms on his shorts and glanced up at the Loco Ladder. "You can do it, buddy!" JJ called.

Tara clapped her hands. "Yeah, go for it, Kevin. You beat this thing at tryouts, right?"

That didn't make Kevin feel much better. Sure, he'd done it once. But the Loco Ladder was hard for him. There were so many things he had to get exactly right, and sometimes his mind just froze up and refused to work with his body.

Still, what difference did it make whether he could do it now? This was just for fun, even if Tara didn't know it yet.

"Okay, here I go," Kevin said. He jumped up and grabbed the pegs.

It was amazing how much easier the obstacle was when he didn't care that much about being perfect. Somehow he landed the pegs in the second set of holes without even thinking about it. His arms pulled him upward, and he made it to the third level just as easily. Only two more levels . . .

He'd just reached the top when a loud gasp almost made him lose his grip on the pegs. He knew that gasp!

"Kevin!" his mother exclaimed. "Is that really my boy way up there?"

Kevin glanced down, his heart thumping with panic. What was she doing here? She looked out of place standing in the gym doorway dressed in the skirt, blouse, and low-heeled shoes she wore to work at the law firm.

He managed to grab the rope dismount and slide to the floor without falling. "What — what are you doing here, Mom?" he asked.

Izzy stepped out from behind his mother. "I asked her to come," she said, her face and voice very serious. "Sorry. But I couldn't just let you quit."

Kevin glared at her. "But I told you —"

"Kevin!" His mother rushed forward, grabbing him by the shoulders. Her face was twisted into an odd expression, and tears were running down her cheeks. "Oh, Kevin. When your friend told me about this, I was so angry, so worried . . ."

Yeah, that was what he'd thought. Some friend! Kevin was so annoyed with Izzy that he almost missed his mother's next words.

"... but seeing you do that just now ..." She waved a hand toward the Loco Ladder. "Well, I don't know what to think! You looked so strong, baby. So confident!"

"We're very proud of how hard Kevin has been working," Tara said, looking a little confused as she stepped forward. "It's nice to meet you, Mrs. Marshall."

"It's Ms. Marshall." Kevin's mother shook the coach's hand, looking a bit confused herself. "And who might you be, young lady?"

Looking more surprised than ever, Tara introduced herself. "I'm coaching the junior ninja team," she said. "Hasn't Kevin mentioned me?"

"No." Kevin's mother frowned, glancing around the gym. "He hasn't mentioned any of this."

"Only because I knew you wouldn't approve," Kevin blurted out. "You never approve of anything I want to do."

"What?" His mother's frown deepened. Normally, that was enough to shut Kevin down, but not this time. It was one thing to not do the show. But now that his mother was here, he was afraid she'd drag him away and forbid him from ever setting foot in the ninja room again. And he couldn't stand that thought.

"I'm sorry, Mom," he said. "But haven't you even noticed that I don't have cancer anymore? I can do stuff like normal kids now. And this is what I want to do. I love being part of this — part of a team."

Mackenzie spoke up. "He's really good at this ninja stuff, Ms. Marshall."

"Yeah," Ty added. "Kev's a natural. Totally."

"The team wouldn't be the same without him," JJ put in.

Izzy nodded, shooting Kevin a sidelong look. "That's why I had to tell her. I'm sorry for spilling your secret, but I didn't want you to miss your chance at being on the show." She cleared her throat and looked away. "It's okay if you're mad, though. I understand."

"It's not this girl's fault," Kevin's mother said. "It's yours for keeping secrets in the first place, young man."

"Sorry," Kevin said again, his shoulders slumping. He should have known there was no way . . .

"And I'm not happy about that," his mother went on. "But if this is really what you want to do —"

"What?" Kevin blurted, hardly daring to believe his ears.

She waggled a finger in his face. "But you be careful, you hear me?" she warned. "Don't take foolish chances." Her gaze darted around the room. "Don't make me regret this."

"I won't, I swear!" Kevin's heart pounded. "Thanks, Mom!"

"Want to stay and watch a little more, Ms. Marshall?" Izzy asked.

Kevin's mother hoisted her purse farther up her arm.

"I would, but I have to get to work. Kevin, don't be late for dinner."

"Yes, ma'am."

Tara walked Kevin's mother out, leaving the team alone. Kevin knew he should say something to Izzy, but he wasn't sure whether to yell at her or thank her.

Before he could decide, Ty cleared his throat. "Dude," he said to Kevin. "That was intense. You were awesome just now."

"You mean the Loco Ladder?" Kevin mumbled, still blown away by what had just happened.

"No—telling your mom how much all this means to you." Ty waved a hand around the room. "It made me realize how much it means to me, too."

"Yeah, ditto," JJ put in.

"No, listen, I really mean it," Ty said. "I just found out I have to choose between doing the show or trying out for my traveling soccer league." He took a deep breath. "And I just decided. I'm sticking with you guys."

"Huh?" Mackenzie blinked. "Wait—you mean you were thinking about dropping out to do soccer?"

"Maybe." Ty shrugged. "But I'm not thinking that anymore. I'm all in. And not just because I want to be on TV, or win." He grinned sheepishly. "I mean, I do still want those things. But I don't want to let the team down, either."

Kevin nodded, realizing he felt the same way. And now he knew what to say to Izzy.

He walked over to her. "Thanks," he said. "I'm glad you told my mom, even though I didn't want you to."

"I felt like I had to, you know?" Izzy shrugged. "I mean, I didn't want you to quit. But I'm not a snitch!"

"I know." He smiled at her. "You're a friend."

Twenty-One

JJ HAD ALWAYS NOTICED when time seemed to move faster or slower than usual. For instance, it slowed to a crawl when he was at one of Jasmine's choir concerts or sitting in math class on a Friday afternoon. But it seemed to rush by at warp speed in the days leading up to the taping of the *Junior Ninja Champion* regional show. Before he knew it, the day had arrived.

"Here's your water, Ty." JJ tossed a bottle to his teammate, who was warming up with some pushups.

The taping was taking place at the state university. The university gym was crowded with other kids doing similar exercises, but Ty had staked out a spot near the locker room doors. The course was set up outside on the college green.

JJ and the others had caught only a glimpse of it so far. Tara had promised to take them out for a better look as soon as they were all settled in.

Ty caught the water bottle with one hand while continuing to do pushups with the other. "Thanks, dude," he said after he took a swig.

Mackenzie peered out of the locker room, sounding panicked. "JJ! Have you seen my sneakers?"

JJ spun on his heel and hurried over. He'd barely stopped moving since the team had climbed out of the van half an hour earlier. Everyone seemed super stressed out and nervous, which made him even more relieved that he was there only to help out and support his teammates. No pressure, just fun, which was exactly the way he liked it.

It had been a long trip to the university — almost three hours on the road, including a stop for a snack at around eight a.m. Ty's parents had taken turns driving the van this time, leaving their employees at home to run the gym while they were gone. Tara was there, too, of course. Mackenzie's dads and some of the kids from school were driving up together later to be in the audience. JJ's family had thought about coming, too. But he'd talked them out of it. After all, he was just an alternate and probably wouldn't get to do anything. Besides, Jasmine had a choir concert.

By the time the Fit Kidz gang had arrived, it was almost nine, and the taping was scheduled to start at ten a.m. sharp. Mackenzie was digging frantically through her gym bag. Kevin sat on the bench nearby, watching her with concern. "What if she forgot to pack her sneakers?" he asked JJ.

"Aah, don't even say that!" Mackenzie cried. "I can't run the course in my flip-flops!"

"You could always go barefoot," Kevin suggested. "Some ninjas do that on *NNC*."

"Hold on. It's okay, let me look," JJ said calmly.

He grabbed Mackenzie's bag and searched it. It was packed with all kinds of stuff, from a whole box of granola bars to a spare T-shirt to several comic books and a stuffed penguin. It had to be the biggest gym bag he'd ever seen. The sneakers were near the bottom, tucked behind Mackenzie's spare laptop. Crisis averted!

As Mackenzie pulled on her shoes, JJ glanced around. "Where's Tara?"

"Signing us in," Kevin said. "She wants to find out the run order so we know when to get warmed up."

"Yeah," Mackenzie put in. "My birth mom says most TV filming is a lot of hurry-up-and-wait."

Just then Izzy rushed over. JJ hadn't seen her since they got out of the van. "Check it out," she hissed. "Someone told me that's the guy to beat. His name's Vince." She nodded toward a kid sitting at the far end of the bench, lacing up his shoes. He was average height but very muscular, with olive skin and a buzzcut.

Kevin leaned forward to check him out. "Good to know.

There'll probably be a lot more competition here than there was at tryouts."

"I bet we can beat them all, though," Mackenzie put in.

"It's not about beating other ninjas, remember?" JJ said. "It's about challenging yourself and just doing your best — or whatever."

"Don't tell Ty that," Izzy joked.

Just then Tara rushed in. "JJ, there you are!" she cried. "I hope you brought your ninja clothes. Because you're on!"

"Huh?" JJ's jaw dropped. Was Tara saying what he thought she was saying?

She grinned. "Some kid from downstate sprained his ankle!" she exclaimed. Then she cleared her throat. "Which is terrible for him. But it means the show needs an alternate to step in, and the producers pulled your name from the list!"

"Awesome!" Mackenzie grabbed her phone and snapped a few photos of JJ's stunned face.

"Yeah." Kevin clapped him on the back. "I'll go tell Ty the team is complete!"

Twenty-Two

"WAIT RIGHT HERE, KEVIN," the producer lady said, steering Kevin over to a little patch of grass just behind the start of the course. "We'll play your package, and then when I point to you, go ahead and step up onto the mat."

Kevin nodded, too nervous to speak. His throat felt dry even though he'd just sucked down half a bottle of water. His palms were so clammy he was afraid they'd slip right off the Ring-a-Ding Swing, which was the first obstacle.

After that he had to get past Stepping Out, which was what the show was calling the balance steps. Kevin closed his eyes, trying to remember Tara's advice from earlier.

They'd spent a good amount of time wandering up and down the course, studying every challenge it offered — and there were a lot of challenges! The eight colorfully decorated obstacles looked much more intimidating than the ones they'd faced at tryouts, especially with dozens of video cameras and huge lights hanging over them on a big metal frame. The competitors weren't allowed to touch any part of the course beforehand, though the producers had sent a few demonstration ninjas through it.

Now the competition was under way, and Kevin was the first of his team to go. In fact, only three other ninjas had competed so far, and none of them had made it past the fifth obstacle. Kevin had watched them as best he could from the warm-up area, but it wasn't the same as doing it himself, or even hearing about it from his teammates . . .

A large audience had gathered outside the waist-high fence that separated the audience from the course. The college green was almost full, and more people were watching from windows and balconies in the surrounding buildings. Some held signs that said stuff like, GOOD LUCK YOUNG NINJAS!

Kevin jumped when the big screen over the announcers' platform suddenly crackled to life. Everyone turned to watch as his smiling face appeared and the package began . . .

"*Kevin Marshall is only eleven years old,*" a cheery announcer voice began, "*but he's already been through things few kids his age ever have to think about. That's because he beat cancer!"*

Kevin felt his cheeks go red as a bunch of people in the audience applauded. He hadn't known that the package was going to mention his cancer! He hadn't said anything about it during his interview the previous week.

Mom probably told them, he thought. *Or maybe Darius.*

He watched as the package continued, showing him working out at the gym and watching *National Ninja Champion* with Darius. Then his mother appeared on the screen.

"I'm just so proud of Kevin," she said. *"I know he thinks I'm too protective. But can you blame me? When he was sick, I was afraid we'd lose him. Now I just never want to let him go."*

Everyone applauded again. Kevin hardly heard them as he stared up at the screen. Were those . . . *tears* in his mother's eyes? Ms. Jacqueline P. Marshall never cried. Never. Even when Kevin was first diagnosed, she'd stayed strong. All those times in the hospital, even the time the doctors had messed up his dose and he'd had to stay an extra week, she'd never shed a tear as far as Kevin knew.

The camera zoomed in on his mom's face, and she wiped away a tear with the handkerchief she always carried but never used. Or did she? Kevin felt a lump in his throat, and suddenly he was afraid he might start crying himself. He blinked a few times, hardly able to see the screen.

A few seconds later he realized that the package was over and the producer lady was pointing at him. His knees trembled as he stepped forward and climbed the three steps up to the mat. Suddenly lots of cameras were pointing at him. The producers had said the ninjas were allowed to wave to the cameras at the beginning if they wanted, but mostly they were supposed to ignore them. So Kevin glanced out at the audience, hoping to catch a thumbs-up from Ty or one of Mackenzie's crazy little excited jump-and-waves. How was he ever going to spot them in the crowd?

Then he spotted two familiar faces — his mom and Darius! They were right there near the start of the course, waving and beaming at him!

Kevin was stunned. They'd told him they couldn't make it because his mother's boss was having a party for new clients and she had to be there. But now he realized the truth — they'd wanted to surprise him. And they wanted to support him, even if they still didn't really understand why this was so important to him. This time he didn't feel like crying at all. Instead he waved back, grinning from ear to ear.

After that, he finally spotted the rest of the team. They were all standing near his family in the little alley that the producers kept clear right beside the fence. As each competitor took his or her turn, that ninja's friends and family were allowed to stand there for a better view.

"Ready when you are, ninja," the producer lady said with a smile.

Kevin nodded and took a deep breath. Then he turned to face the Ring-a-Ding Swing, which consisted of eight rings hanging in a row. He leaped up and grabbed the first ring, using the momentum to reach toward the second one. The rest of the rings went well. Kevin's hands slipped on the dismount rope and he landed a little short but recovered quickly.

Then it was on to Stepping Out, a set of five balance steps, which were painted to look as if animals had left footprints all over them. Third came something called Logging In. It was a log roller sort of like the one in tryouts. However, in this one, there were four logs across. The two logs in the middle were set higher than the outer two, which made it even trickier — like a rolling staircase. Kevin thought he might wipe out on the third log, but somehow he flung himself forward and landed belly-first on the mat. Whew! He'd made it!

The fourth obstacle was the Loco Ladder — Kevin's nemesis. This particular Loco Ladder was painted all over with crazy swirls, laughing mouths, and wildly wide eyes. The decoration was a little distracting, making it hard to see the peg holes, but Kevin did his best to ignore that.

He closed his eyes briefly, remembering the look of amazement and pride in his mother's eyes when she'd seen him conquer the Loco Ladder at Fit Kidz.

"I can do this," he whispered, shaking the tension out of his hands. Then he leaped up and grabbed the metal pegs. They felt solid, cool, and firm in his grip. He didn't wait, jerking one of the pegs out and up.

The peg slotted neatly into the next hole. Kevin didn't pause, yanking out the other peg . . .

Before he knew it, he was at the top. He'd done it! He'd beaten the Loco Ladder!

The crowd went wild as he slid down the rope to the mat. Kevin grinned and gave the audience a double thumbs-up.

The next obstacle was a set of three tire swings. Kevin leaped up and grabbed the first tire. But he was still a little distracted thinking about the previous obstacle, and his hand slipped . . .

"Aargh!" he cried. Before he realized what had happened, Kevin was in the safety net below the tires. Falling hadn't hurt, but it was still a shock to suddenly find himself on his back with the tires far overhead — and his course over.

For a second he was overwhelmed with disappointment. But he shook it off as he saw Tara rushing to meet him, along with some of his teammates.

He gave everyone another thumbs-up as he climbed out of the net. Maybe he hadn't finished the course. But that wasn't the point. He'd just lived out his dream — he'd taken his shot at being a ninja champion! How amazing was that?

Twenty-Three

MACKENZIE SNAPPED A PHOTO of the ninja ahead of her as he started the course. Then she handed her phone to Tara, who was standing next to her in the waiting area.

"Get some shots of me if you can," she said. "Especially if I wipe out in some dramatic way, okay? My blog readers will love it!"

Tara chuckled. "Okay. But they'll love it even more if you complete another course."

"I know. They're calling me the Underdog Ninja. I guess they didn't like the Nerd Ninja nickname I came up with." Mackenzie grinned. She'd been checking the *JNC* website and other blogs and stuff all week. It was amazing how excited people were about the show.

But not surprising, she realized. After all, she got just as excited about following and commenting on all her favorite shows. The difference was, this time she was going to be *on* one of her favorite shows!

"Mack!" Kevin rushed over. "I was looking for you. Watch out for that last ring — it's set a little farther back from the landing than usual. You'll need to make sure you have enough momentum to hit the mat."

Mackenzie nodded. "Got it. Thanks for the tip." She grinned. "And hey, I must be rubbing off on you guys! 'Momentum' is one of my sciencey words!"

Kevin and Tara both laughed. "Good luck," Kevin added. He traded a fist bump with Mackenzie, then hurried away.

Before she knew it, Mackenzie was standing on the mat, waiting to start. Her package started to play, but she didn't pay much attention. She could watch it online later. Instead, she shaded her eyes — the sun was bright overhead — and scanned the crowd. Finally she spotted her dads watching from the alley.

Mackenzie's dads weren't the only ones who'd come to cheer her on. Her birth mom was there, too, along with some other friends and neighbors. Even the owner of the local comic book store had taken the day off to come and watch!

Mackenzie waved and blew kisses to them all. Then she turned to the camera and gave a thumbs-up. As soon as the producer said she could go, Mackenzie leaped up to grab the first ring. Thanks to her teammate's tip she didn't have any trouble completing the obstacle, though there were a lot of rings and her arms were tired by the end.

Getting through the steps was easy, as usual, even though she almost got distracted trying to figure out whether the paw prints on one of them were supposed to be from a raccoon or an opossum. The next obstacle, Logging In, had been one of her favorites when she had checked out the course earlier. For one thing, the stepped heights looked challenging and fun. Besides that, the whole obstacle was decorated with images of keyboards, computers, cell phones, and boxes with letters and numbers typed into them.

"Logging In," Mackenzie whispered with a smile. She got it. And she loved it!

Her feet hit every log just right. Soon she was on the far side, facing the Loco Ladder. She wiggled her arms around, willing her muscles to stay strong.

Calculate and execute, she told herself.

Jumping up to grab the pegs was the easy part. After that, she kept her mind on the exact distance and angle she needed to raise each peg to make it to the next level. She'd learned that if she focused on the numbers, she didn't think

as much about the strain on her muscles. And it worked—
she made it to the top!

She slid down the rope as fast as she could to save her
aching arms. That had been tough! And now she had to use
those arm muscles again to get through the tire swings.

"Getting Tired," she whispered, glancing at the sign
marking the fifth obstacle. It was the perfect name!

She stood on the trampoline for a few seconds to let
her arms rest. But she couldn't waste too much time—the
clock was ticking!

So she bounced twice and then flew up, grabbing the
edge of the first tire. She kicked her long legs out, trying to
get some momentum going. But the tire didn't swing as far
as the ones in tryouts. She would have to jump for it!

She waited until the tire was as close as it could get to
the next one in line. Then she flung herself over, barely
grabbing onto the edge. She looped her arm through the
middle of the tire and hung there for a second, catching her
breath.

"Go, Mack, go!" rang out among the cheers from the
audience. She was pretty sure that was Papa Kurt, though
she didn't dare look down to check. She could hear the
show's announcers on the sound system talking about how
she was doing, but she didn't focus on that, either.

Instead, she locked her gaze on the third and final tire
swing. It looked so far away—how could she reach it, especially when her arms felt ready to fall off?

Then she had an idea.

She pulled her arm out, hanging on to the edge of the second tire with her fingers. Then she started swinging her legs again. This time she aimed right at that third tire. On the third swing, she hooked the edge with the toe of one sneaker!

A gasp went up from the crowd. Most people swung their way from tire to tire using only their arms. But now Mackenzie was hanging between two tires, holding on to the middle one with her hands and the last one by one foot!

That meant she couldn't really see what she was doing now — she was hanging face-down, staring at the safety net below her. Her arms trembled as she fought to hold on to that middle tire . . .

Somehow she hooked her other toe into the third tire, too. Then she took a deep breath — and let go with her hands. That made the tire swing back toward the landing platform. Meanwhile Mackenzie's body swung downward, and one toe started to slip . . . but she jammed it in with all her might and held on until the rest of her body swung all the way down and past the tire as if she were a trapeze artist. Her fingers skimmed the net as her body swung all the way past the tire like a pendulum. As she arced upward on the other side, both toes finally lost their grip, but the momentum of her swinging body sent her flying toward the landing mat . . .

"Oof!" she grunted as she twisted around in midair and

hit the edge of the landing platform with her stomach and chest. The crowd cheered as she managed to hook a couple of fingers through the cargo net and pull herself the rest of the way up onto the mat.

"Wow!" the announcer shouted. "Talk about a dramatic dismount!"

Mackenzie grinned and waved to the crowd. Then she climbed to her feet and stepped off the platform to face the rest of the course. Obstacles seven and eight would be easy — seven was another balance obstacle called Tiptoe Tulips, and eight was the Crazy Cliff. Mackenzie was still the only ninja at Fit Kidz who could beat the cliff almost every time.

But first she had to get past obstacle number six. It was called the Sunbeam. Mackenzie had seen similar obstacles on *NNC*, but she'd never tried one herself. There was nothing like it at Fit Kidz, and there hadn't been one on the try-outs course, either. It was a huge metal beam, shaped like an uppercase I and painted sunny yellow. Ninjas had to hold on to the narrow bottom ledge with their hands and feet and crawl upside down along its length, clinging on like a sloth hanging beneath a tree branch. It looked hard — especially when her arm muscles already felt like jelly!

Still, all she could do was try. She grabbed the ledge, creeping along with as much weight on her feet as she could. But halfway across, one hand slipped and then the other, and her feet came loose . . .

"Oof!" she grunted as she landed flat on her back on the mat.

Mackenzie stood up with a grin, hoping that Tara had photographed her dramatic crash. Maybe she hadn't finished the course this time, but she'd had a blast. She couldn't wait to cheer on the rest of her team — and make sure she got the exclusive interview that Ty had promised for her blog!

Twenty-Four

And now, our third ninja from the little upstate town of Fairview — Ty Santiago, the Power Ninja! You could say that Ty has been preparing for this moment for most of his twelve years. His parents own a gym, and Ty is a star at every sport out there. But now the Power Ninja faces his biggest challenge yet — the Junior Ninja Champion semifinals course!

THERE WAS MORE, though it was a little hard for Ty to hear the recording over the loud cheers from the crowd. But his eyes stayed glued to the video, which showed him shooting hoops at the playground, doing pushups at the gym, and dribbling a soccer ball like a pro. There was also an interview with his parents standing in front of the gym, and a few words from Tara.

Finally the package ended with a shot of Ty powering through a couple of ninja obstacles. *That was awesome!* Ty thought. *This is really happening — I'm on TV!*

As the crowd cheered, Ty smiled and waved to his

parents, who were standing in the alley with the rest of the Fit Kidz team. He felt confident as he turned to face the first obstacle. He'd watched almost every round before his, and he knew exactly what he had to do. Only four kids had finished the course so far, and Ty was sure he could be the fifth. Mackenzie had told him that at least ten ninjas from each semifinals show would move on to the national finals in a few weeks. Ty was determined to be one of them!

"Whenever you're ready, ninja," the starter lady said.

Ty nodded to her, then turned to face the Ring-a-Ding Swing. It was a piece of cake — Ty was through it in seconds. Everyone cheered as he pumped his fist and moved on. Now it was on to the Stepping Out obstacle. He took a deep breath and cracked his knuckles. Then he jumped.

He'd been working hard on balance steps, and it showed. He barely bobbled at all as he skipped from one step to the next. He slipped a little off the last one but stuck the landing anyway.

Then came another balance obstacle, Logging In. Mackenzie and Kevin had both talked to him about this one. It wasn't going to be easy to just power his way across on sheer momentum, as he could when the logs were all at the same level. But he wasn't going to let that stop him.

He leaped onto the first log, barely touching it with one foot before he was onward and upward to the second. But he caught it at an awkward angle, and suddenly he felt his weight shifting too far forward . . .

"Urgh!" he grunted as he flung himself forward, grabbing onto the fourth log with his arms while one foot was still looped over the third. He could feel the logs rolling, trying to chuck him into the water. But he wasn't going to let that happen! He shoved forward, stretching his arms as if he were sliding into home plate headfirst in an important baseball game.

He got it! A couple of fingers looped through the cargo net on the landing mat, stopping him from falling back onto the safety mats beneath the obstacle. Ty used every ounce of upper-body strength to drag himself up and onto the mat.

The crowd erupted into cheers. "That's a Power Ninja for you!" one of the announcers exclaimed over the sound system. "Let's hear it for Ty!"

Ty jumped to his feet as everyone cheered even louder. He smiled when he saw the Loco Ladder next. That was one of the easiest obstacles for him. He shook out his arms, then jumped for the pegs.

He made it to the top in what he was sure was record time. The tire swings were a little challenging, just as Mackenzie had warned, but Ty made it through that obstacle quickly, too. Actually, other than the brief delay at Logging In, he was pretty sure he was making really good time. If he kept up that pace, maybe he could end up winning this whole thing!

The Sunbeam was next. Ty hadn't done anything like it before, but it didn't look too hard. He didn't hesitate, jumping up to grab on as soon as he reached the trampoline mount.

"Ow," he blurted out as he jammed a finger on the hard metal. He'd misjudged the distance a little — he could almost hear Mackenzie now, chiding him about the miscalculation.

But he ignored the slight pain, clinging on with his fingers and heels. His hands almost immediately started to cramp, but he ignored the pain, crawling along as fast as he could. Halfway across, his arms and legs started to shake. This was hard! But Ty wasn't going to let it beat him.

Suddenly his foot slipped. A gasp went up from the crowd as both of Ty's legs dropped. He hung there for a moment by his hands, breathing hard. He needed to find the strength to swing his legs back up there.

Or did he? Ty glanced toward the landing pad. He was at least three-quarters of the way across. If he could swing himself back and forth to gain momentum, maybe he could jump from there.

The crowd moaned as they watched. Ty could hear the announcers talking excitedly as they figured out his plan. But he ignored them. He had to focus.

"Go!" he grunted as he flung himself toward the landing.

For a second he thought he wasn't going to make it. His feet skidded off the edge of the mat, and his body crashed down and bounced off.

But somehow he grabbed the mat with one hand. "Wait — he's got a hold!" an announcer shouted. "Go, Ty!"

Ty gritted his teeth and tensed his muscles, pulling himself up inch by inch, until he could grab hold with his other hand. A second later he was rolling onto the mat, exhausted — but still in it!

The crowd went wild. Ty barely had the strength to smile, but he gave them a thumbs-up. Then he moved on to the next obstacle, the Tiptoe Tulips. That was another set of balance steps. This one consisted of blocks of wood painted to look like flowers. They were stuck on springs that wobbled around when you put weight on them. They looked pretty tough — a lot of good ninjas had failed to make it past them.

Ty felt a flutter of nerves. Balance obstacles were still hard for him, especially ones he'd never tried before. But there were only two obstacles standing between him and the finals show — this one and the Crazy Cliff.

He took a couple of deep breaths and closed his eyes, trying to remember every tip that Tara, Izzy, and the others had given him about balance stuff.

Then he opened his eyes and leaped onto the first block. It wobbled like crazy, and for a second Ty thought he was going down. But he flung himself toward the second tulip and then the third... He wasn't sure how he did it, but somehow he made it through!

"Yes!" Ty whooped in triumph as he felt both feet hit the landing mat.

Already the audience was beginning the familiar chant: "Climb that cliff! Climb that cliff!"

Ty pumped his fist, then turned and started his run toward the Crazy Cliff, eager to join the short list of ninjas who had finished the course.

But when he powered himself up the cliff and his hands stretched for the lip at the top, they came up a little short. A groan went up from the onlookers as Ty slid down the sloped face.

"Aargh!" he howled as he landed at the bottom, so embarrassed that he wanted to kick something. How could he have messed that up? He'd gotten so much better at the cliff lately.

Ty stood up and smacked the wooden obstacle as hard as he could, making his hand sting. He couldn't believe it — one tiny mistake, and his dream was over, just like that!

"Ty!" Mackenzie came rushing up as he left the course. "You looked great out there — really strong and fast! Ready for that interview now?"

"Not now, Mack!" Ty growled, pushing past her and sprinting toward the locker room.

Twenty-Five

HE LOOKS PRETTY GOOD so far," Izzy commented casually. Her eyes were on the ninja currently on course — Vince, the kid she'd heard about before the show started. He'd made it through the first three obstacles in the fastest time yet.

Izzy and Kevin were watching from just outside the starting area. Izzy was scheduled to go right after Vince, and Kevin had just brought her a water bottle.

She took a swig, then handed the bottle back. Kevin took it, though his gaze never left the course. Vince had just dismounted after a successful climb up the Loco Ladder. Now he was moving through the tire swings just as fast.

"Wow! Pretty good?" Kevin said. "He makes the whole

course look like a piece of cake. And I know it's not! I bet some of these obstacles are just as huge as the ones the grownups do on *NNC*!"

He grinned, and Izzy did her best to grin back. But it wasn't easy. She couldn't take her eyes off those tires, hanging so high over the safety net it was dizzying to look up that far. Then she glanced at the Sunbeam, and her mind flashed back to the image of Mackenzie falling from that obstacle, falling down, down, down . . . Her hands were shaking, and her stomach seemed to be doing its best to turn itself inside out. She took another sip of water, but it didn't help much.

"By the way," Kevin said, "thanks again for helping me get here." He had gone all serious now. "I mean it. This was one of the best days of my life, and I almost missed it. Just because I was afraid to tell my mom what I was really feeling."

"You're welcome," Izzy said, distracted. Vince had just started the Sunbeam. Her eyes followed him as he crawled across with hands and feet, high over the pile of mats far, far below . . .

"Hey — you okay?" Kevin leaned closer, peering at her. "You look kind of — I don't know, green around the gills." He smiled. "That's what my nana calls it, anyway."

"I'm fine," Izzy snapped. "Can you be quiet now? I'm trying to focus."

"Sorry." Kevin looked slightly wounded.

Izzy felt bad. He was just trying to help.

"No, I'm sorry," she mumbled. "Guess I'm a little nervous."

"It's okay, I get it." Kevin patted her on the arm. "I was nervous before I started, too. But I kind of forgot about that as soon as I got going. I'm sure you'll be great. You can do this."

"I hope so." Izzy shot Kevin a sidelong glance. He was feeling more and more like a friend all the time. Could she trust him? She hoped so, because suddenly she really needed to talk to someone. "Look, I've never told anyone about this before," she went on before she could lose her nerve. "But the thing is, I'm a little bit, um, afraid of heights."

Kevin turned to face her, looking confused. "Huh? Wait — is this a joke? Because I don't get it."

"No joke." Izzy kicked at the grass. "It's usually not that bad. I'm okay in tall buildings and planes and stuff. It's only sometimes, when I feel like I could fall . . ."

"Like on ninja obstacles." Kevin was nodding now, suddenly looking much less shocked. "That's why you always start off strong on the Loco Ladder and then slow down near the top."

She nodded. "It's also why I'm here at all," she said. "My friend dared me to skateboard down these really steep, high steps. I thought I had it under control. But when I lost my balance a little, I guess I panicked. My board went flying right into a window, and I got in huge trouble."

"Wow." Kevin looked thoughtful. "That's amazing."

Izzy frowned at him. "Not really. I mean, I'm glad I ended up at the gym, but the whole scene was pretty horrible."

"Not that." He waved a hand. "I mean it's amazing that you want to do something that scares you so much. You're really brave."

Izzy was so surprised, she couldn't respond for a second. Just then Tara hurried over. "Ready to go, Izzy?" she asked briskly. "You're up in a sec."

Izzy glanced toward the end of the course. Vince was standing atop the Crazy Cliff, his arms raised in victory.

"He finished?" Kevin said.

"Uh-huh." Tara clapped Izzy on the back. "And so will you, Iz. Let's do this!"

Izzy shot Kevin a look. He smiled and gave her a thumbs-up, and she smiled back. She was glad she'd told him about her phobia. Because just saying it out loud had made it seem much less scary, like something she could beat. She couldn't let her fear stop her from going for it — sort of like how Kevin hadn't let cancer stop him from living his life. If he could do that, she could do this!

She barely listened as her package played on the big screen. As soon as the starter lady nodded, Izzy attacked the course. She flew through the rings and the balance steps. Logging In was fun, and she barely hesitated at the top rung of the Loco Ladder.

Next came the tire swing obstacle. Mounting went fine,

and so did the handoff to the second tire. But on the third, Izzy had to rock the tire back and forth a few times to work up momentum. As she did, she glanced down at the net . . . very far below.

For a second she froze. Then she heard her teammates shouting her name. That snapped her out of it. She flung herself forward, snagging the edge of the third tire with one hand and swinging directly onward to the mat. She almost fell short, but she hooked the net with one hand and pulled herself up.

"Go, Izzy!" someone screamed. Izzy was pretty sure it was Kevin. A second later came a loud whistle — Mackenzie. Izzy squinted past the bright TV lights until she found her teammates in the alley. Mackenzie was jumping up and down with excitement, while Kevin, JJ, Tara, and Mr. Santiago waved and cheered. She couldn't see Ty, but she was sure he was around somewhere.

Izzy smiled. Her family hadn't come to the taping — today was the big charity 10K they were all running in. But that was okay. Her dad actually seemed to feel bad about missing it. And her Fit Kidz family was there to cheer her on.

She took a deep breath and stepped onto the trampoline leading to the Sunbeam. When she jumped up and grabbed it, she realized it wasn't nearly as far above the mats as it had looked. She scrambled across, pausing only briefly to make sure she was ready for the tricky landing.

Then it was on to the seventh obstacle, Tiptoe Tulips.

They were tricky, but Izzy had spent years balancing on a wobbly piece of wood — her skateboard. She made it across, and before she knew it, she was pulling herself atop the Crazy Cliff. Her arms ached and she was out of breath, but she felt great.

"That's two finishers in a row!" the announcer howled over the PA. "Izzy Fitzgerald has done it — great job, Izzy!"

Twenty-Six

JJ WAVED AWAY the water bottle Mackenzie had just offered him. The two of them were in the little waiting area near the start of the course.

"No thanks," he told her. "If I try to eat or drink anything right now, I'll throw up."

"Got a little stage fright, huh?" Mackenzie said with a smile.

JJ blinked at her. It was hard to focus on anything except the fact that soon he'd be out there on course. Just him, with the cameras rolling and everyone watching. Waiting to see what he could do. His heart was beating so hard it felt as if it might burst right out of his chest.

"Stage fright?" he echoed.

"Yeah." Mackenzie tossed the water bottle from hand to hand. "Don't worry, it's normal. I was super nervous before I went, too."

"You didn't look it," JJ told her. "You seemed fine — like you weren't nervous at all."

She shrugged. "Everyone gets nervous before a big moment like this."

"Not everybody." JJ grimaced. "My sister Jasmine loves every second she can get in the spotlight. She's always singing solos and acting in school plays and stuff."

"Maybe. But I bet she still gets nervous," Mackenzie said. "She just knows that the fun part makes up for the scary part."

JJ shook his head, not quite believing that. He'd seen his sister onstage lots of times. She always looked super-confident, as if she never wanted the attention to end.

But what about *before* she went onstage? Now that he thought about it, Jasmine could get awfully cranky before a show. Did that mean she was more nervous than he'd thought?

He was so busy thinking about his sister that he almost missed it when the ninja ahead of him finished. Tara hurried over and shoved him toward the start mat.

"Good luck, JJ," she said. "Do your thing!"

JJ stepped toward the first obstacle. Bright lights were shining down on him even though it was a sunny day. Sweat was running down his face and back. It looked as if a million cameras were pointed in his direction — and a zillion eyes, too. Had more people shown up just to watch his round?

He closed his eyes, not sure he could go through with this. Maybe he could pretend he'd suddenly come down with food poisoning or something. Nobody would want to watch him throw up, right?

"Go, JJ!" Mackenzie's voice floated toward him. "Have fun out there!"

Fun. Was this supposed to be fun? Because right at that moment, JJ wasn't feeling it.

But he'd had a ton of fun getting ready for that moment. Training with his friends at Fit Kidz had been fun. So had the tryouts, at least once he'd gotten over his nerves.

So maybe this could be fun, too . . .

As his package started to play on the big screen, JJ took a few deep breaths. To calm himself, he imagined that he was somewhere more relaxed — like scrambling around in the branches near his tree house. After all, if you took away the cameras and the lights and the audience and the pressure, this course wasn't so different from that. Maybe Mackenzie was right. Maybe it would be . . . fun!

"Whenever you're ready, ninja," the starter lady said.

JJ's eyes flew open, focusing immediately on the Ring-a-Ding Swing. The rings at the gym were one of his favorite things, and he smiled, almost forgetting his nerves . . . almost. As soon as he landed, he gulped as he realized that the balance steps were next. But he pushed aside the flutter of nerves and burst back into motion, leaping from step to step, pretending that the wooden blocks were tree branches. He slipped on the last one and almost lost his balance, but he flung himself forward, just barely reaching the landing mat. Whew! The crowd cheered and he smiled, realizing he was starting to have fun for real.

Almost before he knew it, JJ had made it through the log roller, the Loco Ladder, the tire swings, and the Sunbeam. The Tiptoe Tulips were another hard one, and once again JJ almost lost his balance partway through. But he was looking forward to the Crazy Cliff — ever since he'd finally figured out how to beat it, that had become one of his favorite obstacles. He didn't want to miss out on trying this one. So he dug deep and practically flew over the last two tulip-shaped steps.

"Climb that cliff! Climb that cliff!" the crowd chanted as JJ stepped toward the final obstacle.

He looked up at the Crazy Cliff with a smile. "I can do this," he whispered to himself. "No big deal."

Then he sprinted forward, timing his steps just right as he ran partway up and then flung himself toward the top.

"Yes!" he shouted as he pulled himself upright. "I did it!" He grinned and waved to his teammates below. "Man, that was fun!"

Twenty-Seven

I WISH WE KNEW exactly how many people will make the finals," Mackenzie said for what felt like the millionth time.

The competition had ended more than an hour earlier. Everyone had changed back into their regular clothes. The Fit Kidz van was all packed up and ready to go. The production team had already started to dismantle the course. Most of the spectators had left, including Mackenzie's dads and Kevin's family, who were all going to the gym to set up a post-taping party for the whole gang. Mackenzie couldn't wait to celebrate!

But many competitors and coaches were still hanging around on the college green. The judges were supposed to announce who would advance to the finals, which would take place over Labor Day weekend. That seemed like a long time away, but Tara had explained that it allowed time for all the regional semifinal shows to air on TV.

Mackenzie was trying not to get her hopes up, at least on her own behalf. Her time had been good, but she'd made it only to the sixth obstacle. Lots of ninjas had gone farther than that, so she probably wouldn't make the finals. But you never knew! Besides, she was excited that at least a couple of her teammates would probably make it. How cool was that?

She glanced around the college green. She and her teammates were sitting on a bench in front of a pretty stone fountain. Actually, only she, JJ, and Kevin were sitting. Izzy was balanced on the narrow wall surrounding the fountain, doing spins and jumps. Ty was pacing back and forth nearby like a restless tiger in a cage at the zoo. While everyone was waiting, Mr. Santiago had gone to put more gas in the van. Tara and Mrs. Santiago were a few yards away talking to some other adults.

"How many semifinals shows are there, again?" JJ asked.

"Six," Mackenzie said. "That means there will be kids from all over the country in the finals."

"Just like on *NNC*," Kevin put in.

"Why are you even worried about that, JJ?" Ty sounded

kind of aggressive. "You know you're going to make it—Izzy, too. You both finished, remember?"

"We don't know for sure that we'll make it," JJ said. "But—"

"But I'm the one who should be on that finals show." Ty clenched his fists. "I'm the one with the best chance to win the whole thing!"

Mackenzie traded a worried look with Kevin. Ty still seemed pretty angry about not finishing the course.

Izzy rolled her eyes and jumped down from the wall. "Grow up, Ty," she said. "If you made it, you made it. If not, you can try again next summer."

"And miss another season of soccer?" Ty scowled. "No way. I wish I'd done those tryouts instead."

"You don't mean that!" Mackenzie exclaimed. She'd never expected to become a ninja in the first place, but now she couldn't imagine missing this experience. Not for anything!

Ty didn't even seem to hear her. He was stomping away, and a second later he disappeared into the crowd.

"Yikes," JJ said. "Ty isn't being a very good sport."

"He'll get over it," Izzy said, though she sounded worried. "He's just disappointed. He's used to winning all the time."

Just then the PA system crackled to life. "Attention, ninjas!" a man's voice said. "Attention, please!"

"This is it!" Mackenzie grabbed JJ's hand and squeezed it. "Good luck, everyone!"

Tara came running back over. "Where's Ty?" she asked.

Kevin shrugged. "He wandered off."

"Yeah." Izzy let out a snort. "He's acting like a total baby."

Tara looked concerned. But there was no more time to discuss it. The PA system was coming back on.

"Twelve ninjas from this semifinals competition will advance to the finals in beautiful Southern California," the announcer said. "Here are the names . . ."

Mackenzie was already doing some quick math in her head. "We won't get in," she whispered to Kevin. "But Iz and JJ are a lock! Only nine kids finished."

Kevin nodded, looking disappointed, but not surprised. "What about Ty?" he whispered back.

"I'm not sure," Mackenzie admitted. "It depends on his time. A bunch of ninjas made it to the cliff but couldn't get up, so if he was the fastest, maybe . . ."

She glanced around, but Ty was still nowhere in sight. Meanwhile the announcer was reading the list of finalists, beginning with those who'd finished the course. Mackenzie cheered loudly when he read Izzy's and JJ's names.

When the announcer reached the end of the list, he still hadn't called Ty's name. "Those are your finalists," he said. "We're also asking three alternates to come to the show in case anyone has to drop out. Those alternates are Ty Santiago . . ."

Mackenzie cheered so loudly that she barely heard the other two names.

"Good! Maybe that'll make Ty a little happier," Kevin said.

"I hope so," Mackenzie said, crossing her fingers. This day had been so amazing that she hated to think of Ty being upset. "Look! There's Mr. Santiago," she added. "I guess it's time to go home."

Twenty-Eight

TY STARED OUT THE WINDOW as the van sped down the highway. His teammates had been chattering nonstop since they'd left the university fifteen minutes earlier. But Ty didn't feel like talking. That was why he'd taken a seat by himself in the last row.

"We'll have to fly to the finals show," Mackenzie told the others. "California is way too far to drive."

Izzy laughed. "Yeah, we'd have to leave right now to get there in time."

"Wow," JJ said. "We're going to fly? I've never been on a plane."

"Really?" Kevin sounded amazed. "Never?"

"Never, ever. I swear." JJ crossed his heart.

"My dads already said they'd pay for my ticket to the finals even if I didn't make it in," Mackenzie said. "It's my birthday present. They're going to come, too, and we'll go on a short vacation afterward since school doesn't start until the next Wednesday."

"That sounds cool. I don't know what my mom will say." Kevin sounded worried. "She might not think it's worth it if I'm not competing."

"You have to come!" Mackenzie exclaimed. "I'm sure she'll let you go if she doesn't have to pay for your plane ticket, right? Maybe we can hold a fundraiser or something."

"You can have my ticket," Ty spoke up with a frown. "I'm not going."

"What?" His father sounded startled. He glanced at Ty in the rearview mirror. "What are you talking about, son?"

Ty shrugged as everyone else turned to stare at him.

"Ty, you have to go!" JJ exclaimed.

"No, I don't." Ty didn't meet anyone's eye. "I didn't make it."

"But you're an alternate," Tara said. "Look where that got JJ!"

"Whatever," Ty muttered.

"No, this is serious." Izzy yanked off her seat belt, then spun around to kneel on the seat and glare at Ty.

"Izzy!" Ty's mother exclaimed. "Seat belt back on—now!"

Izzy frowned, then obeyed. But she kept her head twisted around so she could keep glaring at Ty. "You can't wuss out now," she told him.

"I'm not," he protested, annoyed by her attitude. "You were there. I didn't make the cut!"

"I'm not talking about wussing out on the show," Izzy said. "I mean wussing out on the team!"

"Yeah," JJ added quietly. "We need you there, man. *I* need you there."

Mackenzie nodded vigorously. "I never would have made it through the rings in tryouts if you hadn't warned me how slippery they were," she said.

"And you're the one who helped me figure out how to beat the Loco Ladder," Kevin said.

JJ smiled at Ty. "You helped make all of us better and stronger."

"That's the real reason you're the Power Ninja," Mackenzie put in.

Tara was watching them all from her seat near the front. "Face it, Ty," she said. "You're a key part of this team."

"Whether you like it or not," Izzy added with a smirk.

Ty scowled at all of them. But he couldn't help thinking about what they were saying. Was it true? Okay, maybe he had given his teammates a few tips—just like Izzy had shown him her technique for the log roller. Or like Mackenzie had blabbed so much about angles and friction that she'd finally gotten them all up the Crazy Cliff—most of the time, anyway. Or like Tara had coached all of them through their weaknesses as well as their strengths . . .

Not that I have any weaknesses, Ty told himself automatically. *That's why I was supposed to be the champion!*

But then he shook his head. Maybe that was the problem — he'd been looking at this as a sporting event. A contest with just one winner and lots of losers. But was that the only way to look at it? Was it the *right* way to look at it?

"You don't really need me there," he muttered uncertainly. "I mean, you'll do fine even if I don't go."

JJ shrugged. "But we *want* you there."

"Yeah," Mackenzie agreed. "It wouldn't be as much fun without you."

"Without the whole team," Izzy finished.

Ty thought about that. These four kids weren't who he'd expected to have on his team when he became a ninja. But now he couldn't imagine doing any of this without them — *all* of them. And maybe that meant he couldn't imagine ditching them now just because he hadn't made the show.

A tiny smile crept onto Ty's face before he could stop it. "You want me there that much? Really?"

"Really," the others chorused.

Ty's smile got bigger, with a hint of mischief. "Okay, suckers," he said. "Be careful what you wish for. Because I'm going to make sure this team is the best it can be before that finals show — even if I have to lock you in the gym from now until then!"

"Really?" Mackenzie bounced up and down in her seat. "Does that mean you're coming to the finals show after all?"

Now Ty grinned for real. He pumped his fist in the air. "California, here we come!"

Twenty-Nine

MACK ATTACKS . . . . . .

MY BLOG ABOUT INTERESTING STUFF

By Mackenzie Clark, age 10½, nerdgirl extraordinaire! (← *that last word means fab!*)

Today: MACK ATTACKS . . . . . . *Junior Ninja Champion!!!!!!!!!!!!!!!!!*

Wow, it's been a huge day! I'm about to fall asleep, but I just had to update you guys first. I just got back from the taping of my *Junior Ninja Champion* semifinals show, and it was amazing!!!!!!!!!!!!!!!!!!!!!!!!!!!!!!!!!!!

Sorry, I can't tell you about everything that happened

(yet). I can't even tell you (yet) how I did myself. We had to sign all kinds of papers saying we wouldn't spill the beans before our show airs on TV. I'm not sure yet when that will be — there will be six semis shows before the big finale. I'll be sure to update this blog when I find out when mine will be on.

But one thing I can tell you: It was a GREAT experience! My team was amazing, and we can't wait to see what happens next!

Stay tuned . . .

Q&A WITH NINJA
ALLYSSA BEIRD

After many years practicing gymnastics and many months of hard work at ninja gyms, Allyssa Beird competed on seasons eight and nine of the TV show *American Ninja Warrior*. She hopes she can inspire others to face their fears, overcome obstacles, and never give up. Allyssa lives in Massachusetts, where she teaches fifth grade and works on her ninja skills.

Q. How did you get involved in the ninja world?

A. I had seen the *American Ninja Warrior* show a few times on TV and always thought it looked pretty cool. I remember thinking, *Wow, I could probably do some of those obstacles!* Then, during the summer of 2015 when my sister was in town visiting, we decided to check out a local ninja gym and see what it was all about. I was immediately hooked. I was terrible at every obstacle I tried, which was both frustrating and motivating, because I thought I'd be a pretty naturally talented ninja with a background of fifteen years of gymnastics. I started going to the ninja gym every week, and soon added more and more days into my training. I loved training with other ninjas, and I loved getting to compete in local competitions with them! Before I knew it, I was applying to season eight of *American Ninja Warrior,* and soon after I got "the call" to be on the show!

Q. What are your favorite — and least favorite — obstacles?

A. My favorite obstacles are, maybe surprisingly, the ones that took me months to conquer: the Salmon Ladder and the Warped Wall. The Salmon Ladder is fun because there are so many ways to switch it up: going up, going down, transferring between the rungs you're on and the ones behind you, flips between the rungs, and what's known in the ninja world as the "Wilczewski Whip" (named after the ninja veteran Chris Wilczewski): You start with your hips on the bar and "whip" the bar up and behind you, followed by a transfer to the rungs across from you.

The Warped Wall was very frustrating before I conquered it. However, I'm now challenging myself to see how many successful Warped Wall runs I can do in one minute!

Almost every obstacle can be turned into a fun ninja challenge.

My least favorite is the Cliffhanger. The Cliffhanger has a variation of ledges attached to a wall that you move across using only your grip strength. Think of trying to maneuver across the top of a door frame with only your finger strength! It just . . . hurts. Some Cliffhangers have a thicker ledge and are less painful on your fingers than others, but in general your fingers will hurt. I'm getting better and better at the Cliffhanger the more I practice and go rock climbing to build up my finger strength and hand calluses, but it's probably at the bottom of my list of favorite obstacles.

Q. Why did you decide to audition for *American Ninja Warrior*?

A. It's funny — I almost didn't apply at all! The application questions and application video for season eight were due at the beginning of January 2016. In November or December of 2015, it felt like the idea of being on the show was a far-reaching goal. *Maybe next year,* I thought. *After some more training.* However, after some of my ninja friends encouraged me to apply, I (quickly) made my audition video, filled out the application, and then waited . . . until MAY! The five-month wait resulted in getting the much-anticipated "call" from the producers: "We'd love to have you compete in Philadelphia for season eight!" I'm pretty sure I cried on the phone, then cried when I called my closest ninja friend, Jesse Labreck (she was waiting for her call too), and I probably cried when I called my family as well! It was a very emotional day.

Q. How has your ninja life affected your work as a teacher? How have your students responded?

A. The biggest impact my ninja life has had on my teaching life is the ability to be a student all over again and remember what it's like to struggle with something and fail—over and over and over again. I forgot how frustrating it was to see other people around me easily do the things I've been working so hard to do. I was able to relate a bit better to my students, and can now say, "Hey, you know what? I know what it's like to feel like you're giving it a hundred and ten percent and not succeeding. I know what it's like to see everyone around you successfully doing something you just cannot yet figure out. And you know what? This might take a while, but if you keep working at it, it'll be THAT much more rewarding once you succeed!"

Perseverance, motivation, and problem-solving are things I use all the time in my ninja life, so I can use some great ninja examples in the classroom to model these ideas. My students have really enjoyed hearing about any connections I can make between the ninja world and the classroom world. It's also a lot of fun to create ninja math problems and ninja stories, and I've even had students challenge me to arm wrestling!

Q. Can you share any training tips?

A. Of course! During my first year of training, I was really focused on specific obstacles: how to hold the cannonballs (hanging holds you swing across), how to move my lower body when I'm on the Cliffhanger, how to do the Salmon Ladder, how to space out my steps on the Warped Wall, etc. It's important to figure out what your strengths are, as well as your weaknesses, and use all of that knowledge to train the way YOU need to train. My gymnastics background gave me some pretty good upper body strength, so things like the cannonballs, rope swings, and anything involving using my arms came a little easier for me. However, I didn't have a ton of leg power, so I realized I needed to do a lot more work with leg strength if I wanted to be more successful at things like the balance and agility obstacles, the Warped Wall, and my speed through a course.

In training for season nine, I realized I needed to switch up my training to do more non-ninja things, too. I'm bouldering at the rock climbing gym a lot more often, I'm working on sprint drills on the track, and I'm still going to the ninja gym a few days per week.

The most important training tip, however, is to train with people who will motivate you and want to see you succeed, as well as being that person for others. I owe so much of my ninja success to my training friends and fellow ninjas! We're all in this crazy sport together and want to see each other get better and better each day.

Q. Any other general advice for kids interested in practicing their ninja skills?

A. Even if you don't have a ninja gym at which to train, you can practice ninja moves anywhere (just make sure you're safe, and don't try anything you've never done before without a spot or proper padding)! Playgrounds are one of the best places to practice your ninja skills. How many times can you go back and forth on the monkey bars without coming down? Can you lache on the monkey bars (hopping both hands at the same time from one bar to the next)? How quickly can you get across a wobble bridge? Can you climb the fireman's pole with just your hands?

If you have a ninja gym near you, check out their ninja kids programs! It's always more fun to train with other ninjas, so finding a group of kids who also want to practice their skills is a great way to get better. Even though it's still pretty cool to train on your own outside a gym, having a coach, new and creative ninja obstacles, a ninja family, and lots of mats under your feet are always pluses!

Q. What is the best thing about being a ninja?

A. I think the best thing about being a ninja is getting to see your training progress month after month, and realizing that all of your hard work and perseverance pays off! Thinking back to how much I was not able to do at my first ninja practice, all the way to the present day, where I've competed on two seasons of *American Ninja Warrior,* is a pretty awesome feeling! I wouldn't have been able to do any of this without my amazing and supportive ninja family. This sport wouldn't be nearly as exciting and rewarding without the wonderful ninja community. What's also great is that anyone can become a ninja! All you have to do is take your first step into that ninja gym, ready to take some risks, fall a lot, and meet some other ninjas working toward the same goals you are. Happy ninja-ing!

To learn more about Allyssa and her ninja journey, visit allyssabeird.com.

NEXT TIME ON

JUNIOR NINJA CHAMPION

THE FASTEST FINISH

IZZY, HEADS UP!" Kevin said. "We're supposed to do pull-ups now!"

Izzy snapped out of her thoughts. The others were scrambling toward the pull-up bars while she was still in mid-lunge. "Sorry," she muttered.

"Mind in the game, Iz," Tara said. "Being a good ninja is mental, not just physical."

"I know, I know." Izzy jumped up and grabbed a free bar, grunting as she did her first pull-up. Exercises like this, which relied almost totally on upper body strength, were a lot harder for her than the balance or agility stuff, so for the next few minutes she didn't have much energy to spare worrying about Jess.

Tara had just ordered them all to move on to the climbing wall when Mackenzie rushed in, pink-cheeked and out of breath.

"Sorry I'm late again!" she cried. "But you'll forgive me when you hear the huge news."

"What is —" Ty began.

But Mackenzie didn't even let him finish. "There's going to be a wildcard show!" she exclaimed, clapping her hands. "Isn't that amazing?"

"A what?" Izzy said. She had no idea what Mackenzie was talking about.

"What's a wildcard show?" JJ added.

"It's like an extra show — *JNC* is such a huge success that they want even more kids to be a part of it," Mackenzie said. "It works like this . . ."

MACK ATTACKS . . . . . .
MY BLOG ABOUT INTERESTING STUFF

By Mackenzie Clark, age 10½, nerdgirl extraordinaire! (← *that last word means fab!*)

Today: MACK ATTACKS . . . . . . Wildcard Ninjas!!!

Big news, loyal readers! So I already posted what a big hit *JNC* is. But I just found out something even **more** amazing.

The producers want to make the finals even **bigger and better**. So they just announced that they're adding a wildcard show!!!

What's a wildcard show, you ask? Well, I'm going to tell you! It works like this:

1. In two weeks, there will be another day of tryouts in all the same locations as last time — which means one of them is right down the road in North Creek again, where my teammates and I tried out.
2. The course will be different from last time, since the producers assume some of the same people will try out again. (Though nobody who actually made the semis is allowed to try again even if they didn't make the finals — they want to give new people a chance.)
3. A bunch of ninjas will make it through to the wildcard show. It's going to be a little different from our semis shows, since it will tape at all six semifinals locations, but the show's editors will combine it all into one show. Complicated, right? But that way all the wildcard ninjas from across the country can compete against each other — the courses will be identical in all the locations, and Mellie Monroe can still host them all, thanks to the wonders of technology, ha ha!
4. They're expecting tons of people to try out this time, since the show is way more famous now — everyone is watching!

5. The best ten finishers from the wildcard show will advance to the finals competition on Labor Day weekend — just like the top ten ninjas from each of the original semifinals shows. **EXCEPT** . . .

6. . . . if there aren't ten wildcard ninjas who score better than the lowest-scoring finalists from the original semis, then the alternates from those shows get called back for the finals instead. (Which means my friend Ty still has a great shot at competing! Whoo!)

7. So that makes the finals even bigger and better and more awesome!!!! I can't WAIT to see what happens!

ABOUT THE AUTHOR

CATHERINE HAPKA will never be mistaken for a ninja, but she has published more than two hundred books for kids in all age groups from board books to young adult novels. When she's not writing, Cathy enjoys horseback riding, animals of all kinds, reading, gardening, music, and travel. She lives in an old house on a small farm in Chester County, Pennsylvania, where she keeps three horses, a small flock of chickens, and too many cats.